"SOMETHING'S WRONG WITH YOU," IVERSON MUSED.

His eyes raked over her face, looking for a clue to her inner feelings.

"Of course something's wrong with me," Melissa replied. "I'm disappointed. I had planned on our having the day together."

"I do have to earn a living," he said impatiently.

"Do you think I'm a fool?" Melissa blazed, her anger out of control. "I know better than that. How dare you lie to me! I know Nicole called you. She's the one you're going to meet."

Incredulously Iverson's eyes widened and darkened. "You listened in on my call!"

"No, I was in here when the phone rang and I picked it up to answer it. And I want you to understand this. I'm not going to compete with your ex-wife for your attention." She walked to the door, closing her hand over the doorknob. "What else haven't you told me, Iverson?" she asked quietly, not waiting for an answer. "Instead of business, it's pleasure with Nicole."

CANDLELIGHT ECSTASY ROMANCES®

PASSIONATE ULTIMATUM

Emma Bennett

A CANDLELIGHT ECSTASY ROMANCE®

Published by
Dell Publishing Co., Inc.
1 Dag Hammarskjold Plaza
New York, New York 10017

Dell ® TM 681510, Dell Publishing Co., Inc.

Candlelight Ecstasy Romance®, 1,203,540, is a registered
trademark of Dell Publishing Co., Inc., New York, New York.

ISBN: 0-440-16921-6

Printed in the United States of America

First printing—November 1984

To Our Readers:

We have been delighted with your enthusiastic response to Candlelight Ecstasy Romances®, and we thank you for the interest you have shown in this exciting series.

In the upcoming months we will continue to present the distinctive, sensuous love stories you have come to expect only from Ecstasy. We look forward to bringing you many more books from your favorite authors and also the very finest work from new authors of contemporary romantic fiction.

As always, we are striving to present the unique, absorbing love stories that you enjoy most—books that are more than ordinary romance.

Your suggestions and comments are always welcome. Please write to us at the address below.

Sincerely,

The Editors
Candlelight Romances
1 Dag Hammarskjold Plaza
New York, New York 10017

CHAPTER ONE

Melissa Phillips looked up as her employer, Linda Bowman Cresswell, stepped into the doorway of her office. Melissa smiled, taking off her hornrimmed glasses to reveal large, honey-gold eyes that twinkled mischievously in her small pixyish face.

At forty-nine Linda was a beautiful woman. Her hair, naturally dark, was just beginning to streak with gray, and she was slender and carried her clothes well. Simply dressed in a white tailored blouse and a green linen suit, Linda made Melissa proud that this professional-looking career woman was also her mother.

"Time to go?" Melissa asked, gazing fondly at the older woman, glad to see that the anxiety lines were disappearing from Linda's face.

Linda nodded. "You won't change your mind about going with me?"

"I can't. I need to go over the timesheets for the Gerrick account and get it straightened out. That man's gone through more employees in the past two weeks than he has suits. Personally I'm beginning to think he's impossible."

She lifted her hand, running her fingers through her sun-kissed brown hair. Then she stood, flexing her tired shoulders as she slipped out of the tan blazer that complimented her beige blouse and matched the stripes in her tailored slacks.

"It's not turning out like we had hoped," Linda lamented softly, leaning against the doorframe, watching Melissa drape her jacket over the back of her chair. "All this work and it doesn't look like we're going to get his endorsement after all. Instead, it looks like he's going to besmirch our reputation."

"Whether we get Gerrick's endorsement or not," Melissa said, regretting her previous remark, "Day's Work is still the best temporary employment agency in Asheville. In fact, it's the best one in the entire state of North Carolina. And nothing he can say or do will discredit us. Don't worry, Mom," she added softly, "I promise we'll make it with or without his help."

Linda laughed bitterly. "How can you make such a statement, Melissa? The man's gone through our entire list of eligible employees for that position. We have no one else to send!"

Sitting down again, Melissa shuffled through the clutter on her desk. Looking at her mother and grinning triumphantly, she picked up one of the files and waved it in the air. "There's one more! Grace Johnson. She seems to be exactly what Gerrick is looking for, but if she can't please the man"—her eyes flashed with determination—"then I'll go work for him myself."

"I don't know if there is any pleasing Iverson Gerrick," Linda muttered. "It seems like the more we try the less we succeed." She smiled then and changed the subject, saying, "Come on, Melissa. You need to get away from this for the weekend."

Melissa shook her head. As much as she wanted to spend some time with her stepsister, Penny, Penny's husband, Charlie, and her two nephews, she couldn't leave all this work behind. "Not this weekend, Mom."

"We'd love to have you come."

"I know," Melissa murmured, thinking about her stepsister's family. Penny, Charlie, Randal and Lane.

8

Randal, the seven-year-old, looked just like his mother, with big blue eyes and black hair. Lane, on the other hand, had his father's brown eyes and ash-blond hair. Like their father, Charlie, however, both kids were going to be tall and slender. And like Penny, both were warm and loving. Melissa sighed. "There's nothing I would rather do than go with you, but"—she looked up at her mother—"I need the time to myself so that I can think, and *you* need to be away from me and the office."

"SeaCo?" Linda guessed, remembering the long distance call Melissa had received earlier in the day.

Melissa nodded. "Harold called. Les has transferred to the New Orleans office, and Harold wants me to come back to work at SeaCo in Les's position."

"That's wonderful," Linda replied quietly, her heartbeat slowing, her breath catching in her lungs. The moment she had been dreading had arrived much sooner than she had anticipated. She reached up to brush her fingers through her softly waved hair. "Are you going back?"

"Probably not, but I promised Harold that I wouldn't turn him down flat without giving it some thought. So"—she smiled, rubbing her fingertips over her cheekbones, lightly touching the sprinkle of freckles across her nose—"I'm going to give it a little thought while I'm working on the Gerrick account this weekend."

Although Linda wanted to persuade Melissa to stay in Asheville and manage Day's Work for her, she wisely kept silent. She had hoped that Melissa would accept the partnership she had offered her, but she knew she had to let Melissa work out her own future. Quickly she said good-bye and left the office to meet her stepdaughter and her family.

After Linda had gone Melissa put her glasses back

9

on, picked up her pencil, and leaned over her desk, once again trying to work on the accounts. But she couldn't. She had too much on her mind to concentrate on figures. Too many unanswered questions. Could she pull Day's Work out of the red? Could she salvage the Gertick account? Should she return to Galveston and to SeaCo, or should she stay and become her mother's partner at Day's Work?

Although she had been happy the past few months working with her mother, Melissa had to consider all she was turning down if she refused Harold's offer. After eight years, working up from word-processing clerk to office manager, she was elated that Harold would consider her for the position that Les Strader had just vacated.

And, Melissa noted with a slight smile, Harold had not been remiss in pointing out that since Les had been a major factor in her leaving, his transferring should guarantee her coming home. But Melissa suddenly realized that Galveston wasn't her home anymore. Nor did she want to return to SeaCo. Surprisingly Les's transferring hadn't made the difference. The difference had come from within herself, a decision she had unconsciously been making during the short time she had been here in North Carolina.

She twirled the pencil through her fingers, remembering Les, once again seeing his thick blond hair, his familiar blue eyes, his tall, lanky physique, remembering when they had first met. Although they had known each other, they hadn't begun dating until she had been promoted to office manager, working directly under him. From the beginning they had liked each other, and their friendship, which had developed further as he trained her, quickly turned into an office romance.

At first it had been exciting and fun because Melissa

10

had been flattered to receive the attention of a SeaCo executive, and she had enjoyed being with Les. But the excitement died as the newness wore off, and their relationship became dull and boring. The longer they dated, the more possessive Les had become and the surer Melissa was that she didn't want to marry him. Les wouldn't listen to her, however, and he tried to pressure her into making a commitment as he smothered her with his affection. It wasn't enough that they spent all day together; he demanded all her free time too.

He refused to understand that she didn't return his feelings, and he began to make her feel guilty about wanting a life of her own. After she had broken up with him, he had resorted to a subtle type of harassment that left unbearable tension between them. She couldn't stand being cooped up in the same office with him all day long, every day.

It was the telephone call from her stepsister, Penny Blake, however, that had transformed Melissa's life and had pulled her out of the rut she was in. Melissa had known that her mother had been devastated by the death of her second husband, Brian Cresswell, but until Penny had called, Melissa hadn't known the depth of Linda's despair. She was neglecting herself and had completely abandoned the employment agency Brian had started. Penny had suggested that Melissa take some time off from work to visit Asheville.

But Melissa had other ideas. She had known that a change was inevitable in her life; she just hadn't known what kind of change. Nor had she known when she would make the change. But after Penny's call she knew. She would move to Asheville. She soon found, though, that making the decision had been the easy part. The hard part was telling her father and her stepmother, Thekla, both of whom advised her not to leave Texas.

But three months ago Melissa had arrived in Asheville, temporarily moving in with her mother. Linda had been overjoyed about Melissa's arrival, and between Penny and Melissa's attention and encouragement, Linda had come out of her depression and had taken a renewed interest in her life and in Day's Work —the temporary employment agency she and Brian had owned. Now Melissa managed the agency and Linda had drawn up the legal papers for Melissa to become a partner.

Still, Melissa reasoned, even though Linda could handle the business, she just couldn't abandon her mother. Then she realized it wasn't just a matter of abandoning Linda; she herself didn't *want* to leave Day's Work. She wouldn't be doing Linda that great a disservice if she left, because her mother was a fighter. And without her here, Linda would be forced to put all her energy and concentration into Day's Work. But, as Melissa had come to recognize, this was her home now. She cared about Day's Work, and she wanted to fight for it. She wanted to save it.

Knowing what she must do, she picked up the telephone and began dialing SeaCo, confident that her decision was the right one. She wouldn't be returning to Galveston to live or to work because her future was here in Asheville.

After she had talked with Harold, Melissa hung up the phone and for a long time gazed out the window, looking at the mountains that peaked into the blue sky. How quickly events changed, she thought. Harold had just offered her the position she had once coveted with all her heart. Yet she had turned it down with no regrets.

She turned away from the window and her eyes saw

the Gerrick Corporation timesheets which seemed to be mocking her. Today she believed Iverson Gerrick to be the devil incarnate. Yet just two weeks ago she had thought him a godsend. She remembered how she and her mother had danced around the office, giggling and acting like children as they celebrated getting the account. Until then, Linda had been dealing solely with small companies. With this account they had hoped to prove the worth of Day's Work first to Asheville, then to the world.

Meticulously Melissa had gone through their records, searching the profiles of each of the people they kept on file, looking for the right fill-in for Mr. Gerrick's assistant, remembering every detail Gerrick's private secretary had told Linda. He's hard to please, Ramona Swinson had said. *We've been through five agencies already. Send someone who's qualified. Send a mature person. An older person preferably. Send someone who's presentable since she'll be attending public meetings and conferences with Mr. Gerrick until his assistant, Jarvis, returns from his two-month vacation.*

So Linda and Melissa had searched, and they had sent their best; but one by one each woman had returned with battle scars, swearing she would never again work for Iverson Gerrick or for the Gerrick Corporation. The man is a beast, each had declared vehemently. Physically handsome, they admitted, but also heartless, callous, and overbearing. He was altogether too demanding. He expected them to be as familiar with his routine as he was. He gave them no instructions, and he allowed them no time for learning.

The voice of the receptionist, Bonnie Carson, drifted through the open door, breaking into Melissa's troubled thoughts. "Call for you on line one."

Glancing at the clock, Melissa laughed. "Who would call me at five-thirty on a Friday afternoon?"

"Iverson Gerrick," Bonnie Carson returned, appearing in Melissa's doorway.

"Iverson Gerrick or his secretary?" Melissa quizzed.

"Him," Bonnie answered.

"That's a first," Melissa mused. "Usually Ramona is the one who calls. Did he ask for me personally?"

Bonnie shook her head. "No, he asked for the owner."

"Did you tell him that Linda wasn't here?"

"Yes, but that didn't satisfy him. He demanded to speak to the manager."

Melissa chuckled, slipping into her jacket. "Well, I'm not one of the owners *yet*, but I'm the manager."

"So you ought to talk with him," Bonnie said.

Melissa had no intention of talking with Iverson Gerrick. A conversation between them boded no good, and she didn't want to begin her weekend on a sour note. "Can't you ask him to call back Monday morning?"

"Can't. He won't listen to me; he's out for blood."

"I hate to get caught in the middle like this. Mom's always talked with him before." Silently Melissa implored Bonnie. "Are you sure you can't put him off until Monday?"

"No way," Bonnie returned, backing out of the room.

"Okay." Melissa sighed, watching the retreating figure as she leaned across the desk, her hand curling around the white telephone receiver. "I'll take it." She lifted the phone and laid it against her ear, saying in her most pleasant voice, "Hello, Mr. Gerrick, I'm sorry but—"

Not even allowing Melissa to finish her explanation,

Iverson Gerrick interrupted her. "I don't have time for apologies or small talk, lady. I'm a busy man, so let's get down to business."

"And I'm a busy woman," Melissa snapped, wishing Mr. Gerrick's temperament were as melodic as his voice. "It's Friday afternoon, and we're closed for the day, so I, too, would appreciate it if you'd get right to the point." But remembering the reputation of the agency, she softened the hardness of her angry retaliation. "Just how may I help you?"

"That's an understatement if ever I heard one," he sneered. "I don't think you have the ability or the talent to help me. One more week with help like your agency has given me this past week and Gerrick Corporation will be permanently damaged."

Totally undaunted by the power that Iverson Gerrick wielded, Melissa tensed in her chair and drew a deep breath, preparing herself for battle. Tactfully sweet, with just that touch of saccharinity to let him know how she felt, she said, "I know that you haven't been pleased with any of the employees I've sent out, Mr. Gerrick, but I'm not sure that I understand why. Please tell me."

Readily he complied, and Melissa listened, acknowledging his list of complaints. She inwardly seethed until she silently exploded, but outwardly she remained calm, never letting the man know the depth of her fury.

"Come Monday morning," she articulated softly, her hand tightly gripping the receiver, "I'll send a woman to your office who is the *paragon* of all that you've mentioned, Mr. Gerrick. Perhaps more!" Her voice dripped with honey as the cogs of her mind quickly spun around, formulating a plan.

"You have a lot of gall. What makes you think you have another Monday?" However, Iverson Gerrick

15

waited for no answer as he continued to lambaste her. "You advertise specialized service. I believe the term you use is *quality* service in the areas of administration, bookkeeping, word processing . . ." On and on his voice thundered as he insultingly read aloud Melissa's brochure. "So far I haven't seen any of these employees, because you've sent me women who were incapable of doing simple clerical jobs."

"We do have quality employees," Melissa defended heatedly, "and I guarantee that we do have one who will suit you, Mr. Gerrick." Her voice dropped to a murmur. "Even if I must come myself."

"Oh, God, spare me, lady!" he exclaimed venomously. "If there's anything I don't want, it's your stupidity down here at my office."

Melissa couldn't have hated Iverson Gerrick any more than she already did. She despised him for making her beg and she despised herself for having to beg, but she was determined that she would save this account at any cost. Biting back her anger and pushing aside her pride, she asked, "Would you please give Day's Work another chance?"

"Why should I?"

"Surely," Melissa began in a placating voice, "we have the right to redeem our reputation."

"All right," he purred arrogantly, sounding pleased with himself. "I'll give you *one* more chance. But don't bother sending anyone for the temporary administrative position, and please don't come yourself. Just send me a typist." He stopped and laughed abrasively. "Based on the past performance of your agency, I won't even ask for a good typist. But, mark this, if the one whom you send should prove to be as bad as the others you've sent, I won't hesitate to let other businesses know what I think about your company."

"You would ruin our company's name?" she gasped in horror.

"No, I won't ruin your company's name. I won't have to. You're doing a fantastic job of that yourself. I'll just tell the truth about the services you advertise but can't deliver." He gave a laugh that sounded almost sinister to Melissa. "Well, let's just see what next week brings."

At the close of the conversation Melissa slammed the receiver into the cradle and slumped over her desk, Iverson Gerrick's hateful laughter echoing in her ears. She was glad her mother had already left for the weekend. At least this would be one less worry for her.

As Melissa leaned back in her chair, she vowed revenge. Iverson Gerrick's amusement and sardonic laughter were nothing compared to the pleasure she would get when she brought him to heel. And she would.

CHAPTER TWO

Monday morning Melissa walked across the parking lot toward the Gerrick Building. She had explained her plan to her mother last night, and they had argued about the wisdom of her working for the Gerrick Corporation, but Melissa had been adamant in her resolve. Rather than send another employee to face Iverson Gerrick's wrath, she would go herself. She could see what was going on there, and she'd be the "perfect" employee. Linda had worried about an angry retaliation if he should learn Melissa's identity, but Melissa had quickly explained that he would have no reason to suspect that she was Linda's daughter.

After Linda's divorce from Melissa's father, Clive Phillips, she had begun using her maiden name, Bowman. And even after her marriage to Brian Cresswell, she had retained the surname Bowman for professional reasons, thereby keeping her private life and her business life separated. Therefore, Iverson Gerrick would never know that Mrs. Brian Cresswell, Melissa's mother, was also Linda Bowman, the proprietor of Day's Work. He would never know that Melissa was the woman he had spoken to on the telephone on Friday.

Gloating over her ingenuity, Melissa walked proudly, holding her head just a little higher than usual. Although her heart thumped with apprehension, she was excited. She would please Iverson Gerrick if it was the last thing she did, and no matter what he dished out, she wouldn't turn tail and run.

With bold recklessness she was challenging the man, and with the impetuosity that often landed her in difficult situations, she was reacting. She also was aware that she was overreacting to the man's fiery temper and his false accusations, but she was exhilarated at the thought of proving him wrong.

Catching a glimpse of her reflection in the tinted glass in the entryway, Melissa examined herself. She didn't look matronly, but she had attempted to dress conservatively. A beautiful white silk blouse with a high, round neckline complimented her brown suit. Her only accessories were tiny gold earrings, her wristwatch, the brown leather handbag that hung from her shoulder, and her brown thick-soled walking shoes. She had attempted to comb her hair into a smooth bun on the top of her head, but the silken strands rebelliously slipped out of the confines of the hairpins, hanging around her face in sun-spiked beauty.

With a haughty toss of her head she confidently walked into the large suite of offices marked Gerrick Corporation, and announced herself to the receptionist, who nodded and gave her directions. Slowly Melissa turned, moving down the corridor, looking at the names on the desks and doors. Finally she stopped in what looked like the main office of the typing pool— the area for which she had been hired—and she glanced first at her wristwatch then at the large clock that hung on the wall. She was puzzled. Here she was thirty minutes early, yet all the desks were filled.

She was certain her clock-in time was nine-thirty because Ramona Swinson had called Linda at home late last night to tell her about the last-minute change.

She wondered why the woman had called with the time change, but she and Linda had been too busy discussing her scheme to even question Ramona's action. Now it was too late, so Melissa shrugged aside her nagging doubts as she walked down the long aisle toward the desk. She stopped and smiled at the woman who sat there.

"Hi, I'm Melissa Phillips. Ms. Swinson is expecting me."

A grimace wrinkled the older woman's countenance, but she never looked up from the word-processing keyboard she was typing on. Crisply she replied, "Ms. Swinson *was* expecting you. Now Mr. Gerrick is expecting you." She lifted her left hand and pointed toward the door behind her, her eyes never leaving her word-processor. "If you'll just go in there." With no further explanation her hand returned to the keyboard, and she dismissed Melissa, never missing a tap on the keys.

If circumstances had been different, Melissa would have laughed at the entire situation. As it was, she swallowed her surprise and looked at the large oak doors that menacingly loomed in front of her. She stepped around the desk, and when she was closer to the door she read the name plaque: IVERSON GERRICK. Her hand curved around the wrought iron pull, and she gave a tug, the heavy, ornate door whisking smoothly over the light-gray carpet.

She stepped inside the spacious office, but no one was at the desk. She paused for a moment; then she heard a noise from the inner office. Quietly she walked across the room, turned the doorknob, and entered an even larger room. She took one step and stopped dead in her tracks, staring at the man who stood behind the desk. At the sound of her entry he had lifted his head, and he, too, stared at her.

Transfixed, Melissa was unable to move. With a brutal jolt she realized that she hadn't been prepared for Iverson Gerrick, and she intuitively knew that this was he. His eyes were the same russet color as his hair, and he was solid muscle from shoulder to feet. He wasn't tall, but he was stocky, which made him seem strong and powerful.

The craggy contours of his face reminded her of a piece of roughly hewn granite. Beautiful stone, she thought, but hard and unfeeling. Never had she been so aware of such blatant masculinity before. Not even the trappings of civilization—the white long-sleeved shirt, the exquisitely designed tie, or the brown business suit—could diminish the force of virility that exuded from this man.

"May I help you?"

The question was polite, almost civil, but not friendly. Still, despite the thread of irritation that laced the words together, the husky vibes were as pleasant this morning as they had been Friday evening when he had called Day's Work, and now Melissa found herself rendered speechless by the sheer presence of the man. Iverson cleared his throat, emphasizing his impatience. "May I help you with something?"

Finding her tongue, Melissa said, "I'm Melissa Phillips from . . . Day's . . . Work."

Her words slowly droned to a halt as she saw disapproval etch itself deeply into his features. The russet eyes were wary; they studied her; they carefully perused her. And although the red-brown depths had an autumnal beauty, Melissa could find no warmth in them. They were icy and aloof.

"Ah, yes," he said quietly, turning to his desk, tossing down the paper he was holding, his voice as chilly as his eyes. "My typist from Day's Work." With an indolent casualness in his movement he lifted his left

21

arm to gaze at his watch. Then he raised his face to hers, a full smile on his lips. But again there was no friendliness there, only mockery. "Day's Work is going out of its way to impress me, isn't it? However, this kind of impression is going to cost your employer a tidy sum, miss."

Melissa arched her shapely brows, taking another step into the room, her shoes sinking into the thickness of the carpet. "I'm not sure that I understand you."

"Why are you an hour late?"

"Late? Your secretary told my—" Melissa barely caught herself before she blundered. Under no circumstances must she let him know that she was Linda's daughter. "I must have misunderstood Ms. Bowman."

"How gracious of you to accept the blame," Iverson returned scathingly. "I wasn't sure whether I should blame the ineptness on the firm or on the person whom they sent." His lips twisted sardonically.

"It's not the firm's fault," Melissa said dispiritedly, wondering how the rest of the day would go with such an inauspicious beginning.

"I'm not sure that I would be so willing to take the blame for a mistake like this one," Iverson mocked. "From my dealings with Day's Work I've gotten the impression that the name is a misnomer. I've gotten anything *but* a day's work from any of the employees whom they've sent. But the employees can hardly be faulted," he said magnanimously. "The fault lies with the owner."

"From what I know of Ms. Bowman," Melissa said, barely keeping her temper under control, "she's trying her hardest to please you." She looked directly into his russet eyes.

"How kind!"

"Maybe I'm just a kinder person than you are,"

Melissa grated, straightening her back and jutting out her chin.

"I don't think so," he mused quietly, admiration gleaming in the hard eyes. "I have a feeling that underneath all that sweet, tender exterior there breathes a real live spitfire."

Melissa's lips curved into a full smile, and she chuckled softly. "No, Mr. Gerrick, you're the one who's spitting fire. Not me. I'm simply a firefighter." When he made no angry outburst, she continued. "If you'll just show me where I'm to work, I'll get started." She turned toward the door. "You wanted me to type?"

"No," Iverson began, "I really don't want you doing any work for me. I've already called Day's Work and canceled my contract, and I'd just as soon that you'd leave, Miss . . . uh . . . Miss . . ." He hadn't forgotten her name, but he knew that it usually irritated a woman to think that she had made such a slight impression on him that he couldn't remember her name.

Having played this game before, Melissa watched him with a scornful glower. She wouldn't make things any easier for him than he was making it for her. "No, Mr. Gerrick, we're not going to call it quits. You can cancel your contract effective tomorrow, but you owe me a day's work, and I want just that—a day's work." This time she smiled. "If you don't give it to me, I'll be forced to turn you into the labor board."

"You don't frighten me with your idle threats," Iverson told her, his mouth twisting into a bitter grimace, "but I'll give you a day's work. But remember this, little lady, you're going to be docked for a full hour and a half. The day starts at eight. I won't pay for time that you didn't work." Her aggressiveness irritated him. "I don't intend to pick up the bill for the ineptness of that firm for which you work."

Melissa chuckled at him. "I'm sure that Ms. Bowman will be more than happy to pay me for this hour, Mr. Gerrick. I'm sure that she will be woman enough to admit her mistake in misunderstanding the time that was stated." Melissa lowered her voice and murmured, "Your secretary couldn't have made the mistake when she called Ms. Bowman last night to confirm the clock-in time, could she?" She kept her lips curved in that sweet, innocent smile. "No, probably not. It would be impossible for your firm to have made the mistake, wouldn't it?"

"I didn't make a mistake, Ms. Phillips!"

Iverson didn't smile, but the icy gaze in his eyes began to melt, and the russet orbs began to twinkle, reminding Melissa of the leaves on the trees in the autumn, fluttering in the wind, glistening gold, brown, and red. Whether he liked her or not, he grudgingly admired the woman who stood so defiantly in front of him. He almost smiled when he saw the triumphant glow in her golden-brown eyes as he spoke her name.

"Your coming here at nine-thirty isn't really the biggest mistake that your employer has made," he continued, his voice low and sweet, the tone belying the full impact of his words.

"Pray tell, Mr. Gerrick, what is her biggest mistake?"

"Having sent you!" A physical blow couldn't have packed a more deadly wallop than his softly spoken exclamation.

"Me!" Melissa gasped. "Why me?"

"That's what I've been asking myself ever since you walked in," Iverson retorted smugly. "You're not what I asked for." His eyes quickly scanned her petite form, lingering on the plain, thick-soled shoes that detracted from her overall sophisticated appearance. "Not at all."

Melissa stilled the anger that billowed inside her. Taking a deep breath, she walked until she stood in front of his desk. "How do you know that I'm not what you asked for? You can't possibly make that judgment until you've seen an example of my work."

"I can make that judgment, Ms. Phillips," he refuted her "and I do. When I talked with the manager of Day's Work on Friday afternoon, she promised to send me exactly what I asked for. I believe, in her words, she promised to send me a *paragon of virtue.*"

Careful to keep her voice quiet and submissive, Melissa didn't correct him. All she had promised was a paragon. Instead, she said, "If you'd give me a chance, Mr. Gerrick, I can prove to you that I'm exactly what you need." She laughed softly. "When Ms. Bowman recited your specifications, she didn't mention my virtue, but I assure you, sir"—Melissa lowered her face and slowly batted her eyes—"even though I'm not a paragon of virtue, I can muster up enough to qualify my working for Gerrick's."

Iverson couldn't prevent his smile from surfacing, and he couldn't keep from thinking Melissa Phillips was a spunky little devil. He did, however, keep the warmth from fusing into his voice. "I didn't say that I asked for a paragon of virtue. I said your employer promised me one." This time the russet eyes slowly ran up and down her length, making her tingle from head to toe. "Come to think of it," he mused, "I don't want you to muster up any virtue at all." He lifted his face and looked squarely into hers. "I'm seriously considering giving you the chance, Melissa Phillips, to prove to me that you are exactly what I need."

Melissa couldn't pretend to misunderstand his insinuation, but she, too, marshaled all her control and kept the telltale color from seeping into her cheeks. Looking him square in the eye, she said, "Thank you, Mr. Gerrick, I'm sure you won't regret your decision."

"I hope not," he murmured, his eyes intimately sweeping over her. Then, lifting his face, he suddenly asked, "How old are you?"

Melissa blinked her eyes in surprise and stared blankly at him. Of all the gall! she fumed, her face growing red with her indignation. "Old enough to know better, but—"

Iverson stopped her in midsentence, shaking his head. "Uh-uh. I'm in no mood for worn-out clichés. Just tell me your age."

"Why?" Melissa demanded coolly. "Are you planning to discriminate on the basis of my age?"

"I don't discriminate. I simply asked you how old you were. Got a chip on your shoulder because you're a woman?"

"No, I don't have a chip on my shoulder because I'm a woman," she mimicked, her humor as usual surfacing at the wrong time and place, causing her to give an unwise retort. "But I do have two lumps on my chest because I'm a woman." Her golden-brown eyes twinkled, and she caught her breath when she saw the flicker of more than interest in his eyes. "Now, tell me why you're suddenly so interested in my age?"

He laughed. "Put it down to simple curiosity. I wondered what Day's Work considered to be maturity. You see, I did specify a mature person." Sparks of fire glinted in his russet eyes.

"And surely, Mr. Gerrick, you should know that maturity is not based on years. It simply means that something or someone is fully developed. And I can assure you that I am."

Now his face creased with amusement, and the in-

26

terest in his eyes was glowing like red-hot embers.
"Perhaps Ms. Bowman knew exactly what she was
doing," he murmured, sitting down in the large
leather chair. Although his lips curled into a sensuous
smile that exposed beautiful white teeth, the sincerity
of the gesture never reached his eyes. "I've always had
a penchant for fully developed . . ." His sentence
drifted off into a whisper, and Melissa had to lean
forward to hear the last word. "Women."

The smile of appreciation widened on Melissa's
face, and she found herself enjoying the sensuous web
that Iverson Gerrick was spinning around her. She
was intrigued by his sardonic humor and good looks.
She was mesmerized by his deep, husky voice and by
his insinuations. She had to admit that he was a first
for her. Never had she met anyone who seemed so
determined to be as disagreeable as he did.

She smiled, gladly playing follow-the-leader with
him, at the moment not even thinking about where it
could lead her. "I don't know what your taste in
women is, Mr. Gerrick, but I guarantee you that I can
handle any job." She paused for effect, knowing what
she was doing. "And I can handle it well." She slowly
wet her dry lips with the tip of her tongue, her heart
pitter-pattering in her chest so fast and so loud that
she thought surely he could hear it.

He threw back his head and laughed, this time the
sound pleasant to Melissa's ears. He waved his hand at
the chair that was placed in front of his desk. "Won't
you be seated, Melissa." It wasn't a question; it wasn't
a request; it was a command. "I'd like to discuss your
qualifications with you if you don't mind."

"And if I do?"

"We'll discuss them anyway." Iverson dismissed her
question with the same wave of his hand.

"I thought as much," Melissa murmured softly, not

minding the discussion but resenting Iverson's over-bearing and arrogant attitude. She sat down, slid her purse strap from her shoulder, and lay her purse in her lap. She lowered her head, running her hand down her thigh, smoothing the wrinkles out of her straight skirt. Then she lifted her face to his, her honey-brown eyes peeking innocently through the stylish frames of her glasses. "What would you like to know?"

Iverson pushed back in his chair, placing his elbows on the armrests, bridging his fingers in front of himself. "Tell me why you think you're the answer to my problem. Why do you assume that you're the one person I need for this job?"

"I'm not the person you need in the typing pool," she quietly confessed, her eyes locking with his, the honesty of her declaration knocking the wind out of him momentarily.

"Why are you here then?" he demanded, prickly because she had the ability to throw him off course.

"Oh, don't worry," she told him, tickled because he couldn't quite categorize her. "I'm quite capable of handling it, and I'll probably do as good if not better job than any of your more experienced personnel. But I'm really the person to be your administrative assistant while your permanent one is on vacation."

"My administrative assistant!" He whistled almost noiselessly. "That's quite a mouthful. Why such a high aspiration for the employee of a temporary agency who was sent as a typist?"

Melissa's eyes glowed, golden rays splintering through the irises, and she leaned forward in her chair excitedly. "I'm glad you asked me that, Mr. Gerrick, because the answer to your question is the one characteristic that separates Day's Work from other temporary employment agencies. Our staff is made up of men and women who are highly trained, skilled, and experienced in their areas of expertise. They are working for us—" A slip of the tongue. But she noticed in that split-second that Iverson didn't take the use of the pronoun as personal to her. Still, she quickly amended her sentence.

"Many of the women are working for Day's Work because they want to get away from the house occasionally, but, at the same time, they don't want to be full-time employees. Most of the men are semi-retired, also wanting only temporary work. In order to get people of this caliber, Day's Work has to pay them more, and although the agency does provide clerical employees, we focus primarily on the more highly skilled worker." Her speech over, she leaned back, taking a deep breath.

Unimpressed by her description, Iverson said, "Had it not been for the manager's insistence, I wouldn't have hired even a typist from Day's Work, but she begged me for a chance to redeem the agency's reputation. I agreed to give it another chance, but I'm going through another agency to fill my administrative assistant's position until my permanent employee returns."

"But why should you?" Melissa asked, again leaning forward in her chair, her palms beading with perspiration. "I fully qualify, and I'm already trained." *Even to the degree of working with a bear like you,* she mentally noted. "Are you interested?"

Surprisingly he seemed to relax, and he crossed his arms over his chest, grinning and cocking his head to the side. "I'm interested, Melissa Phillips," he told her, his eyes again suggestively moving over her body, lingering on the gentle swell of her breasts. "I'm definitely interested. Convince me."

She couldn't keep the heat from flushing her face a dull red. She didn't like the double meaning to his statements; she didn't like the intent that glimmered in the deepness of those auburn eyes. She knew his interest was compelled and motivated by sheer curiosity or at the most by male lust. And she knew he was pushing her, trying to get her to lose her control. But she would play this game by his rules until she had chalked up enough points to be the winner. And all the while she would enjoy the game.

His grin broadened. "I'm waiting, Ms. Phillips."

When Melissa spoke her voice was even and smooth, betraying none of her irritation. "First of all, I have my MBA, my areas of expertise being office management and computer science. Second, I was office manager for SeaCo for eight years, directly supervising a typing pool that consisted of twenty people and working as the aide for the undervice-president of the company." She sat back in her chair, and to cover her mounting tension, she smiled, looking into his face, her gaze never wavering. When he refused to break the silence, she suggested, "With a minimum amount of training and of frustration on your part, you will have a fully qualified assistant if you hire me."

Iverson swiveled around in his chair and brought his hands up, locking them behind his head. As he stared out the window at the majestic outline of mountains across the horizon, he asked, "What kind of work were you doing?"

"Import-export."

"Where? You don't sound as if you're from around here." He turned his head and looked at her.

"I'm not," she agreed with a short laugh. "I'm from Galveston, born and bred a Texan."

"The woman I spoke to on the phone on Friday had a Texas drawl too."

"That's how I came to Day's Work. She's a relative of a friend of mine back home."

He nodded, rising to his feet. "I'm going to get a cup of coffee. Would you like to have one?"

"Yes, please," she answered, calling over her shoulder as he walked from the room. "Do you need me to help you?"

"No," he replied from the kitchenette that adjoined his office. "Just tell me how you want it."

"Three teaspoons of sugar and enough milk to color it creamy."

She heard the soft rumble of laughter, and she smiled even though she knew he was laughing at her. The sound was pleasant and delightful, and it lacked any of his previous ill humor or sarcasm. She could sense that he had believed her story about knowing the manager and he seemed to be more relaxed. She was startled when she heard his footsteps on the carpet, and she saw the cup that he held in front of her. With awkward movements she reached up and took the cup, unable to keep her fingers from touching his.

As their fingertips grazed, she lifted her face, and both of them looked into each other's eyes, each mesmerized with the other. At that moment both recognized the potential for a deeper relationship to develop between them. Whereas Iverson openly endorsed such an idea, Melissa refused to consider it seriously. She dropped her gaze from his and she looked at his thick fingers that were lightly splayed with auburn hair.

"Here you are, Melissa Phillips," the deep, husky voice announced. "One cup of coffee with three teaspoons of sugar and enough milk to color it creamy."

Melissa giggled quietly, taking the cup into her hand and sipping the hot liquid before she said to the retreating figure, "You're laughing at me again, Mr. Gerrick."

He sat down in his chair, setting his cup on the desk, and as he shrugged those massive shoulders, Me-

31

lissa saw the muscles ripple beneath the white shirt that was tautly stretched across his torso. "Perhaps it's like the old adage, Melissa. I'm not laughing at you; rather, I'm laughing with you."

Melissa slowly shook her head, the silky strands of glowing brown hair wisping around her lower face and neck. "No, Mr. Gerrick, you're laughing *at* me—not with me—because I'm not laughing."

"But I'm not making fun of you," he confessed softly. "I was—" He broke off because he couldn't speak the words that hovered so close to the opening of his lips. He had been laughing and teasing with her because he liked her; he enjoyed their verbal scrimmage. He had laughed because she made him happy.

"You were what?" Melissa prompted, unconsciously leaning forward, watching the expressions that played across his face, softening the rugged contours.

"I was laughing because I was enjoying you."

Melissa's breath caught in her chest, and she lowered her head, unable to keep the soft color of pleasure from seeping into her face. She cradled the coffee cup in both hands, and she gazed at the creamy liquid, not wanting Iverson to read her thoughts.

Glad that she had lowered her face because he didn't want his thoughts revealed either, Iverson continued to gaze at her. For that one small minute he had been happy, and he had reacted naturally and spontaneously with Melissa. His action surprised him. During the years since his divorce from Nicole he had built an impregnable wall around his emotions that not even the most beautiful or alluring women had been allowed to penetrate.

Yet this woman, so unpretentious and unassuming, had innocently put him at ease. In just the few mintues since she'd been sitting in his office, she had dispelled the heaviness from his shoulders; she had been like a ray of sunshine on a dark, cloudy day. She wasn't beautiful, he thought. She wasn't even pretty. But she was more than that; what she had was deeper than superficial beauty. She was fresh and fragrant like the great outdoors. She was warm and glowing. There was an aura of vitality about her that he wanted to capture, to hold, and to have as his. It was these thoughts that frightened Iverson Gerrick.

"Melissa," he finally said, deliberately breaking the silence and destroying the intimacy he had created, "I want to ask you a question, and I want a straight answer." He gazed directly across the room and waited for her to lift her face so that they were looking into each other's eyes. "Why are you working for a temporary agency like Day's Work when you could have a much higher-paying position?"

Melissa struggled to give him an answer that would be truthful yet wouldn't tell him more than she wanted him to know. In an effort to think through her reply, she lifted her cup to her lips and sipped her coffee.

"Why don't you want to talk about it?" he prodded. "Something pretty bad happen to make you leave Galveston? Something perhaps that would keep you from having good recommendations?"

"I wasn't fired, if that's what you're getting at. I resigned my position with the company, and I can get excellent recommendations from any of my supervisors."

"But there's something," he pursued relentlessly. "I just can't put my finger on it."

"I really can't see that it's any of your business," she retorted quietly, reaching up to brush the fringe of hair on her forehead, memories of Les rushing to the forefront of her mind. "I'm not asking for a permanent position with your company. I just want to be

33

your temporary administrative assistant. And my life is my own and has been for the past twenty-nine years." Although her face was expressionless, her voice was firm with purpose. "I think you've ceased talking about my qualifications and have begun meddling in my private affairs."

"Maybe," he agreed, "but a lot is at stake. Your coming in here as a typist, asking to be trained as my administrative assistant, which is definitely not the position I had in mind for you—"

"For me in particular," Melissa interposed, "or for the employee whom you requisitioned last Friday?"

Iverson leaned over his desk, unable to break Melissa's penetrating gaze. For countless seconds they stared at each other, neither speaking. Eventually he said, "If I'm going to hire you, Melissa, I think I have the right to know something about you."

"I'll tell you anything you need to know about my qualifications for this job, but my reasons for having left Galveston are personal." She would tolerate no further infringement. Standing up, she walked to Iverson's desk, picked up the telephone receiver, and held it toward him. "If you'll just dial the number I'm about to give you, you'll reach SeaCo. You can ask for the personnel department and they will vouch for me." She held the phone in his direction. They knew she had left for personal reasons and wouldn't give away her affiliation with Day's Work.

His hand closed around the receiver, but rather than putting it to his ear, he laid it into the cradle again. "Okay." He sighed. "What more do you want to tell me?"

"Nothing. Nor do I want to play Twenty Questions. I'm tired of games. I don't mind an interview, but I strongly object to your prying into my private life."

"If you're not running from your job, perhaps you're running from someone."

"Guess all you want," Melissa granted him, spinning on her heel, and walking toward the door.

She was irritated because he had partly guessed her reason for having left Galveston. But unlike Iverson thought, she wasn't running from Les, nor was she running from unrequited love. She was racing toward her future, seeking her destiny and her happiness, none of which included Les. But she didn't owe Iverson Gerrick an explanation.

When her hand closed around the doorknob, she turned, saying over her shoulder, "Now, Mr. Gerrick, I'll say good morning. I can't say that it was a pleasure meeting you, but it has been a unique experience."

"Running again, Ms. Phillips?" he taunted, standing also, quickly moving from behind his desk, striding toward the door.

"I'm not running, Mr. Gerrick. I'm walking out, leaving with my integrity intact. No one has the right to dig into my past or into my privacy without my permission, you included. I don't have to work for you. I'm well qualified, and there are plenty of companies who will be happy to have my services. I don't have to stay here and take this kind of harassment from you or anyone else."

He winced, replying in cool tones, "I didn't realize that I was harassing you, Ms. Phillips. I was simply protecting my interests."

"At the expense of mine."

"One thing I've learned this morning," Iverson told her, "is that you're overly sensitive." When Melissa opened her mouth to refute him, he held his hand up in a placating gesture. "But we'll let it drop, Ms. Phillips."

"*We'll* let it drop!" she repeated heatedly, her hands

35

on her hips. "I've never picked it up to drop it, Mr. Gerrick. You're the one who's been running around with a shovel, digging up my past, trying to uproot me. You're the one to drop it, not I."

Genuine amusement glowed in his russet eyes, and a smile twitched at the corners of his lips. "Okay, Ms. Phillips, I give up. I concede victory to you, on your ground, on your terms. I'll drop it. Just one more question."

Melissa sighed heavily, shaking her head. "Absolutely no more ques—"

Before she could complete her sentence, however, he laid a finger against her lips. "Do you still want the job?"

Her mouth still open, Melissa stared for only a second before she nodded her head. "Yes, I want it, but I'm not going to grovel at your feet for it."

"Why are you so determined to have this job when, as you pointed out, you can get one with countless other companies?"

"I want to prove to you that I can do it."

"That puzzles me. Why are you so concerned with making a good impression on me? What does it matter to you?"

"I like the owner of Day's Work," Melissa returned truthfully. "She needed help, and I knew that I could give it to her. Since her husband's death, life hasn't held much meaning for her, and she let their agency slowly dwindle into almost nothing. I'm working for and with her in an effort to build it back up."

"And you would like to have my endorsement for Day's Work, so the very best that Day's Work has got is at my beck and call."

"Something like that," Melissa admitted. "And that, Mr. Gerrick, is all that I'm going to tell you. Like it or not."

"I like it, Melissa Phillips," he retaliated, grinning. "That is exactly what I wanted to know. And what I want to know I generally find out one way or another." He gently pushed her away from the door and opened it. "If you'll just follow me, Assistant, I'll show you to your office."

"Do you always put prospective employees through the third degree?" Melissa asked curiously, following him into an adjoining office.

"I'm naturally curious," he returned unperturbed, walking to the windows, rolling up the red roman shade. "I like to know all about the people who work for me."

"Again," Melissa informed him, her eyes glowing with appreciation for the modern beauty of the spacious room, "let me point out: you're not hiring me, Mr. Gerrick. You've employed Day's Work, and I am an employee of Day's Work." She stood behind the desk, running her hand over the satiny white finish. "And though the difference is small, I must remind you, there is a difference."

"I have a feeling, Melissa, that I might rue the day that you and I met. I have a feeling that you will be constantly reminding me of differences."

"Isn't that what an assistant is for?"

Iverson favored her with a small grin. "Wouldn't you like to think so!" Then he asked, "What do you think of your office?"

"It's lovely," she replied. "I really like the colors." Her eyes moved to the white furniture, the cobalt-blue carpet, and the bright reds, greens, and yellows that were splattered around the room in pictures, lamps, filing cabinets, and notebooks.

Iverson stood in the doorway, one hand resting on the doorjamb, the other indolently resting on his hip.

"It looks just like you, Melissa. Bright, cheerful, and sunshiny."

Melissa's face darted up, and her surprise was evident for him to see. "Thank you."

He moved away from the door, and quite suddenly all friendliness was wiped off his face. He was the aloof and distant Iverson Gerrick whom she had met when she first walked into the building. "I want you to meet Ramona. She'll take you around and introduce you. After that I want you in my office with your notebook and pen in hand." He smiled, again that sardonic mockery gleaming in his eyes. "We'll see exactly what you're made of, Melissa Phillips."

"Pretty strong stuff," she quipped.

"Are you?" Iverson taunted softly. "I doubt it, but if you are, it'll take me a little longer to find out why you left Galveston."

"You'll find out why I left Galveston only if I want you to know," Melissa told him. "And only when I want you to know."

Iverson chuckled as he walked away from her. "But mark my words, Melissa. I will find out. Sooner or later."

"And, Mr. Gerrick," she responded quietly, her voice following his retreating figure, "you will learn sooner than later that when I make up my mind, it's made up. You'll find out no more than I wish to tell you." She ran her fingers over the appointment calendar on her desk. "And I don't wish to tell you a thing."

Just before he reached the large oak doors to his office, Iverson turned and looked through her open door, his lips curving into a teasing grin. "But you will before it's all over."

And with a cocky wave and the last word, he disappeared. Melissa stood at her desk, staring at the door.

The man was an enigma to her; one she would probably never understand, but, she reasoned, she didn't want to nor did she have to understand him. All she wanted was his endorsement for Day's Work. All she wanted was to bring him to heel. Or was that *all* she wanted?

CHAPTER THREE

The first month at the Gerrick Corporation was the hardest for Melissa, and no one, not even her mother, knew exactly how difficult those weeks had been. The first obstacle was Ramona Swinson, Iverson's executive secretary. Although Ramona seemed to be sweet and friendly to Melissa's face, Melissa believed this was only a front. Although she couldn't understand why, Melissa felt the power struggle that seemed to exist in Ramona's past, and she sensed Ramona's jealousy. When she continually found herself in trouble with Iverson due to no fault of her own, she began to suspect Ramona of sabotage.

The second obstacle was Iverson. However, Melissa soon learned that her trusted weapons were her ever-present humor, her willingness to learn, and her ability to learn quickly. She never quivered or quailed in front of him when he disapproved of her opinions or her decisions; rather, she stood her ground, quietly discussing the differences, trying to understand his viewpoint, trying to explain hers to him.

The third person at the Gerrick Corporation with whom Melissa thought she would have to reckon was an institution within herself, Orlaine Bromley, executive vice-president of the company. She was a tall woman with gray hair pulled back in a neat chignon on the nape of her neck, and she always wore a dark-colored two-piece suit with a pastel blouse.

On Friday, the fourth week of Melissa's employment with the Gerrick Corporation, the reckoning with Miss Bromley came. Melissa had arrived at the office early that morning so she could get Iverson's material ready for an important meeting that evening. However, she had hardly gotten the papers spread across her desk before Miss Bromley appeared at her doorway.

"Where's my copy of the Davidson file?"

"It should be on your desk," Melissa replied, looking up in surprise. "I left it there."

"I don't think so, Ms. Phillips," Orlaine said briskly, "but I'll look again."

No sooner had Miss Bromley turned and walked away than the telephone rang. Sighing her irritation, Melissa picked up the receiver. "Melissa Phillips."

"Mr. Gerrick would like to see you immediately in his office," Ramona announced softly. "And, off the record, Melissa, I'll warn you, he's quite angry. You should learn to be more careful in the future."

Surprised, Melissa asked, "What's he angry about?"

"You'll find out soon enough," Ramona taunted, hanging up abruptly.

Melissa put down the receiver. Why was Iverson angry? she wondered. She had compiled the Davidson file for Miss Bromley, and she had delivered it to her yesterday; she had completed the Dexter file and had all of the copies distributed. Now she was preparing the data sheets for tonight's meeting. What had she failed to do? Slowly she straightened the papers on her desk, sliding them into their file jacket.

Then she stood, preparing for another fiery encounter with Iverson. She lifted her hands to straighten the collar of her white long-sleeved blouse, and she ran her hands down the sides of her yellow pleated skirt. Before she could leave for Iverson's office, however, Orlaine returned just as the telephone rang again.

"Be with you in a minute, Miss Bromley," Melissa apologized, sitting back down, reaching for the receiver. She knew it would be Iverson demanding to know where she was. As she placed the receiver against her ear, she murmured, "Melissa Phillips."

"Ms. Phillips"—Iverson's angry voice flowed through the line—"where is my copy of the Dexter file? I thought I told you to have it on my desk no later than yesterday."

"I did," Melissa replied, her eyes inadvertently sweeping to the chair where Miss Bromley sat, slapping several files against the palm of her hand. "I gave it to Ramona before I went home yesterday."

"No, Ms. Phillips," Iverson grated impatiently, "you didn't give Ramona the Dexter file. You gave her the Davidson file."

Melissa knew she hadn't given Ramona the wrong file, but she also knew that it was useless to argue with Iverson. She had learned during the past weeks that he would believe Ramona's word over hers. "I'm sorry, Mr. Gerrick. I'll get the Dexter file and bring it to you right away."

"I trust the preparations for tonight are going much better than this."

"Yes, sir. The portfolio is assembled and ready for you. I'm going over the last printouts now."

"Good! How about the dinner?"

"The dinner?" Melissa asked blankly.

"The dinner," he barked. "Don't tell me you've forgotten? Ramona said she told you about it two weeks ago."

"No, I didn't forget;" Melissa murmured. How

could she? she thought. She had never been told about a dinner. A meeting, yes! A dinner, no!

"Why didn't you confirm the reservation with Ramona?"

The reservation! What reservation? What was he talking about? Slowly she said, "I'm sorry, Mr. Gerrick, I didn't realize that it was necessary for me to do so. It was never explained to me that I had to answer to both you and Ramona."

"You don't have to answer to Ramona," Iverson thundered, "but there are certain channels through which we have worked in the past, Ms. Phillips, and I see no reason to change them just to suit you. Jarvis always let me know about his plans through Ramona, and I don't see why you can't follow the same arrangement."

"I will in the future, Mr. Gerrick," Melissa promised him, not offering an explanation of her oversight, but she did add, "Since there has been a misunderstanding about what I've done so far, may I confirm a few of the details for tonight's dinner?"

"I think you better," Iverson said.

"What time are we meeting?" she asked hesitantly.

"Are you sure that you and I are talking about the same dinner and the same meeting?" he asked her impatiently.

"Yes," Melissa returned, "we are. However, if you had given me the instructions directly, Mr. Gerrick, instead of having gone through Ramona, this misunderstanding could have been avoided. The matter could have been handled more efficiently, and you wouldn't have to be so concerned at the last minute. Now, if you'll just answer my question, I'll be able to confirm to your satisfaction that my plans are going according to schedule."

"Seven, Ms. Phillips." He sighed his impatience

again. "Tom and George are meeting me here at the office this afternoon, and we're driving over to the Mountaineer."

Seven o'clock! Melissa thought, her eyes automatically darting to the bright yellow wall clock. Just a few hours in which to make reservations for a party of God-only-knew-how-many at the Mountaineer. And that party included Thomas J. Whitman of Whitman Transportation International and George Dillson of Dillson Amalgamated Shipping.

"Confirmation, Ms. Phillips?"

"Confirmed," Melissa said.

"And already I anticipate your next question."

"You do?" She couldn't hide her surprise.

"I do. You're wondering if you can have the rest of the afternoon off in order to get everything ready."

"That sounds like a winner," she agreed.

"Well, you can. Take off as soon as you check all the material I requested for the meeting tonight, and be sure to wear something besides those Bromley office uniforms."

"Formal?" Melissa asked.

"After five," he told her, paused, then asked, "Is anything wrong, Ms. Phillips? You sound strange."

Melissa forced herself to laugh. "I'm okay. I'm just having a difficult time changing gears, Mr. Gerrick. All morning I've been going over all these stat sheets, the proposal, and job profile, and I was thinking about them."

Her reply seemed to satisfy him. "Tonight's negotiations are very important to me, Ms. Phillips, and I want to make sure that absolutely nothing on my part goes wrong. I consider the dinner a top priority." He laughed. "Because Ramona thought you had forgotten the dinner and because she knew how important this was to me, she was all set to make last-minute arrangements."

"Everything has been taken care of," Melissa assured him calmly. "We will have dinner at the Mountaineer, and there's no need for Ramona to make any arrangements, Mr. Gerrick."

There was nothing more that Melissa wanted to do at the moment than throw her hands up in the air and confess her ignorance about the entire affair, but she knew that her keeping her job with the Gerrick Corporation and the reputation of Day's Work rested on the outcome of this dinner, and Ramona had known it also. Until now Melissa had just suspected Ramona of duplicity; this incident confirmed it.

"Oh, yes," Melissa said with deceptive nonchalance before Iverson could hang up, "I meant to check on this also. I need to call to confirm the number of guests whom we'll be expecting."

"Six," he returned. "Tom, George, Orlaine, you, Dad, and me." He waited until he heard her soft murmur of acknowledgment. "Anything else?"

"Don't be late."

Iverson released a gusty laugh that grated on Melissa's highly strung nerves. "This is one dinner date that I wouldn't miss for all the world, Ms. Phillips. Too much is riding on this one meeting, and one meeting may be all the time I have in which to present this joint-venture proposal. I must convince them." Then on a softer note he asked, "What do you think of the Iverson Homestead?"

"The Iverson Homestead?"

"Oh, that's right," he muttered, recalling Ramona's words. "You couldn't go with Ramona to see it the other day, could you?"

Anger, hot and billowing, raged through Melissa's body, almost choking her as she tried to swallow her outrage. She had never been asked to go; she hadn't known there was an Iverson Homestead. Ramona had plenty to answer for, and at the right time, Melissa promised herself, she would make sure she did.

At that moment Orlaine saw Melissa's features contort in anger; she saw the hesitancy of perplexity turn into the fire of fury. The older woman became more than a shadow in the background. She moved to Melissa's desk, laid her files down, and took the phone from Melissa. "Iverson, I presume?"

"Miss Bromley," he boomed fondly. "What can I do for you?"

Orlaine's deep laughter resounded throughout the room. "Must we always have these business dinners at the Mountaineer?"

"Why not?"

"Why not entertain at the Homestead?" Orlaine countered without answering his question.

"I don't know," he replied tentatively.

"There's more privacy and it's more relaxing for all concerned," Orlaine pointed out. "I think it would be much more profitable in the long run."

"What about the plans that Ms. Phillips has made?" he mused, liking the idea but not wanting to make any alterations that would possibly ruin the evening.

"Easily canceled," Orlaine replied, winking at Melissa. "I'll do it myself."

"What about dinner?"

"Melissa and I will drive out early and help your housekeeper, Estelle." She waited awhile, giving him time to think and to decide. Eventually she asked, "Well, what's it going to be?"

"The Homestead."

"Good," Orlaine replied crisply. "Now hang up so we can have dinner prepared by seven."

Iverson chuckled fondly. "Miss Bromley, you are

probably the only person in the world who could tell me this and with whom I wouldn't argue. Good-bye, and I'll see you at seven." Orlaine dropped the phone receiver into its cradle. "Well, Ms. Phillips, don't you think we'd better get moving if you're going to have dinner ready by seven o'clock?"

Melissa didn't move, nor did she answer. She just looked at the woman. "Why, Miss Bromley? Why are you doing this?"

Orlaine gave Melissa one of her rare smiles that softened her harsh features. "I like you, Melissa, and I have a feeling you've been a victim of our overly efficient Ms. Swinson." She picked up the stack of files she had laid on Melissa's desk. "I have all five copies of the Dexter file, and my copy of the Davidson file is missing." Her smile melted into a quiet chuckle. "But to more important matters. From what I overheard, you are responsible for dinner tonight."

Melissa nodded.

"Then, Melissa, we are wasting time, sitting here twiddling our thumbs and discussing the whys and wherefores. Let it suffice to say that I've had Ramona 'forget' to give me a few of Iverson's messages, and I understand the little"—she paused—"the little witch. Perhaps one of these days Iverson will."

Giggling and jumping to her feet, Melissa hastily gathered her papers together and shuffled them into a file that she put into her briefcase. "I wouldn't be so kind as to call Ramona Swinson a witch, Miss Bromley."

"Ah, Ms. Phillips," Orlaine returned with a belying gravity and somberness, "perhaps I'm just a kindlier soul than you are, seeing that I'm a year or two older than you." She chuckled. "Now, grab your things, and we'll drive to the Iverson Homestead. Are you sure you have everything you'll need for the meeting tonight?"

"Everything," Melissa replied, slinging the strap of her purse over her shoulder. She draped her suit jacket over the crook of her arm and closed her hand around the handle of her briefcase, following Orlaine down the hall.

When Orlaine walked into her office, she said, "While I'm clearing my desk, you give Iverson his copy of the Dexter file, and I'll meet you at the parking lot. Okay?"

"Okay," Melissa sang, almost dancing into Iverson's office, excitement causing her honey-colored eyes to gleam with golden highlights. When she raced past Ramona's desk, her smile was broader than usual. "I have to give these to Mr. Gerrick," she called out, not bothering to wait for Ramona to announce her. "It's the profile and stat sheets for tonight's meeting and the Dexter file."

As her hand closed on the doorknob, she called softly over her shoulder, "Thanks for telling me about dinner tonight, Ramona. That was so kind and thoughtful of you. And I do regret that I was unable to go to the Iverson Homestead with you the other day, but I'm going tonight." With a quiet chuckle she opened the door and disappeared behind the oak panel. "Mr. Gerrick, with your permission, Miss Bromley and I are leaving now." She approached his desk, laying the file down. "And here's all the material that you requested. I also have copies for everyone who will be present at the meeting."

"Good," Iverson responded, nodding his head in approval, picking up the file and flipping through the sheets. Then he lifted his face and smiled his appreciation. "You really seem to have everything under control, Ms. Phillips. I had my doubts at first, but you're

48

proving to be everything that your firm advertised and claimed you to be." He paused briefly and said, "In the future, however, I would like to be apprised of the plans ahead of time."

Warm waves of pleasure washed over Melissa, and she could feel herself becoming red. "Thanks," she mumbled, irritated that his first freely given praise would be over a service that she hadn't rendered and perhaps wouldn't be able to render. But never one to focus on the negative, she smiled brightly and retraced her steps across the room. "I promise to let you know ahead of time next time." Closing the door behind her, she poked her head through the crack, calling, "See you tonight. Do you need me to draw you a map?" she asked, laughing.

His deep gravelly laughter harmonized with hers, and the two were caught in a timeless web of discovery, sensing again that potential for a deeper relationship. "No," he returned, the resonant timbre of his voice sending an avalanche of tremulous passion down Melissa's spine, "not this time. I think I can make it on my own."

Again they stared at each other for that infinitesimal second before she pulled her head out of the door. With a satisfied smile decorating her small, delicate face, she turned to look at a surprised and irritated Ramona. Smugly Melissa sauntered across the room and winked at Ramona. "Have a wonderful weekend, Ramona. I'll see you Monday and tell you all about the dinner."

She closed the door and raced down the hall to meet Orlaine in the parking lot. The older woman followed Melissa to her home and waited while she gathered her clothes and called her mother at work, explaining that she wouldn't be home until quite late that evening.

"Special dinner for Iverson," Melissa said from the bedroom extension as she shed her skirt and blouse and pulled on her jeans and cotton shirt. "Big business deal. We're having dinner at his house."

"This is rather sudden, isn't it?" Linda asked.

"Quite sudden," Melissa returned dryly, launching into a full description of the morning's events, telling Linda about Ramona's duplicity, Iverson's anger, and Miss Bromley's intervention.

When her mother began to vent her anger against Ramona, Melissa chuckled and said, "Now you sound like an old mother hen."

"Not an old mother hen," Linda denied. "Just a mother—and an angry one at that. Also a curious one. What are you wearing?"

"One of the outfits Dad and Thekla gave me just before I left—the ecru lace blouse and the wine-colored skirt."

"Good choice," Linda agreed. "Old-fashioned and romantic. Just the thing for a business dinner."

"Mom," Melissa emphasized, "this *is* a business meeting, nothing more."

"Whether it's a matter of business or a matter of the heart," Linda said, "I want you to impress Iverson Gerrick tonight."

"Believe me, Mom, I'll probably impress Mr. Gerrick very much before this night is over." She thought about the dinner she was to have prepared by seven, not telling Linda about it because she didn't want her mother to worry unnecessarily.

"How would you like to wear Grandma Bowman's cameo brooch, the earrings, and the stole?" Linda asked with sudden inspiration. "It would go beautifully with your outfit."

"Oh, Mom!" Melissa squealed. "I'd love to."

Linda quickly told Melissa where to find them.

Then she said, "Have fun, and take care, darling. Remember to leave me an address and a phone number."

"Will do," Melissa promised, dropping the receiver onto the hook and flying across the room to her walk-in closet, ferreting for her evening bag and for the shoes that matched her skirt. Grabbing a small suitcase, she laid it on the bed and filled it with her clothes. Then she walked into the den, announcing, "Well, Miss Bromley, I'm ready for tonight's fiasco."

"You're not worried, are you?" Orlaine questioned, watching as Melissa moved into the kitchen.

"A little."

"Worried about what Iverson will think about you?"

"Personally no," Melissa replied absently, writing her mother a note. "Professionally yes. I want his endorsement for Day's Work."

When Melissa walked down the stairs of the Iverson Homestead Friday evening to greet Iverson, his two business associates, and his father, Iverson was astonished. He hadn't expected such a transformation. His anxieties fled, leaving on his countenance a look of wonder and awe as a smile slowly spread across his face. His eyes instantly shined with renewed appreciation—and interest in Melissa as a woman.

She moved down the stairs so gracefully and so smoothly that Iverson would have sworn she was floating, and her eyes never left his, her honey-colored irises glowing with a radiant beauty. Her greeting was gracious and warm, including all of them, making them welcome, putting them at ease. She was all that he could have hoped for in an administrative assistant, more than he had dreamed possible in a hostess for an evening.

But tonight she was even more than administrative

assistant or hostess; she was a woman, a desirable woman. As she led the small group into the living room and indulged in conversation, he watched and listened to her appreciatively. Her laughter, rich and spontaneous, filled the room, adding to the warmth created by the huge fire that roared in the stone fireplace.

She was so modern, so in step with the times. Yet she was soft and vulnerable in her beauty. Her hair, swept away from her face in a chignon of curls, looked like a golden halo around her face, accenting her maturity, downplaying her pixyish charm. The lace blouse was romantic and old-fashioned, with its stand-up collar, long sleeves, and ruffles. He liked the wine-colored skirt that hung in deep gathers from her small waist, gently swishing as she walked.

Tom Whitman, a cultured and debonair man in his early fifties, was very much the suave businessman, impeccably dressed in a three-piece suit, his silver-gray hair brushed from his face, his blue eyes keen and alert. Captivated by Melissa, he set out to charm her.

Dillson, too, liked Melissa, and he vied with Whitman for her attention. But he wasn't the kind of man to whom Melissa was attracted. Dressed in a nondescript brown suit, he was a short, heavyset man who constantly chewed on a cigar and who loved to be the center of attention. When he talked he would first run the tips of his fingers over his balding head, then rest his hands on his rounded stomach.

Of the three, though, Melissa liked Bradley Gerrick the best. He wasn't an exceptionally handsome man, but he was distinguished. His black hair was streaked with gray, contrasting beautifully with his black suit. After Iverson introduced his father to Melissa, Bradley visited with her for a long time before he sought out Orlaine Bromley. After that the two of them spoke quietly, excluding themselves from the rest of the group.

The evening progressed smoothly and amicably. The dinner was succulent and well prepared, inviting compliments from everyone. At one point Iverson lifted his head, his eyes catching and holding Melissa's. Raising his glass of wine to his lips, his eyes spoke silently, thanking her for the evening. Just as the rim of the crystal glass touched his bottom lip, he smiled, and Melissa felt her heart catch and skip a beat; she felt giddy and light, her head swimming with excitement. And it wasn't from the wine she had been drinking.

Such a beautiful, sweet moment, to be broken by the crude, raucous joking of George Dillson. "Well, Iverson, I'll say one thing, you've got a fantastic girl Friday." He leaned across the table, his pudgy hand patting Melissa's. "I wouldn't mind having one like her."

Melissa's first impulse had been to jerk her hand free, but she reacted more calmly, her eyes gazing into his faded blue ones. With her free hand she lifted her wineglass to her lips and sipped, barely tasting the wine. Then she set the glass down, slowly withdrawing her hand from under his.

"I am neither a girl, Mr. Dillson, nor am I Mr. Gerrick's girl Friday. I belong to myself solely; I only work for Mr. Gerrick." She smiled sweetly, blinking back the outrage that smoldered in the depth of her eyes. "I may, however, be of some help to you. If you should like to have an employee who's as competent as I am, why don't you try Day's Work employment agency? It furnishes such employees, men and women. But no girls Friday."

Orlaine and Bradley were too involved in their own conversation to have heard George, but Tom Whitman emitted a low, dry chuckle, clearly amused with

Melissa's retort. Because he had always considered Dillson to be crude and uncouth, Tom thoroughly enjoyed seeing him put in place.

Iverson also watched the scene with mild amusement, silently lauding Melissa's refutation. Deliberately he shifted his weight in the chair, and he reached for Melissa's hand, closing his big one around it.

"Some people might see her as my girl Friday, George, but she's not." His lips curved into an endearing smile, and Iverson looked at no one but Melissa. "And if I do have a wish, it would be that she were my girl every day of the week, not just Friday."

George guffawed. "So that's the way of it, is it?" He lifted his wineglass, quickly draining it. "Well, congratulations. I'm happy for you." Then he said, "I suggest that we get down to brass tacks. I've got a lot to do, and I'm ready to hear about this venture."

Under the low murmur of polite conversation, the small group adjourned to the large library. A fire blazed in the fireplace, its flames coating the vibrantly colored carpet in an orange glow, casting beautiful shadows from the bottom of the rich wood-paneled walls to the highest beam that supported the cathedral ceiling. A bentwood rocker was nearest the fireplace and across from it was a contemporary sofa upholstered in soft beige. At the end of the sofa was a large brass lamp sitting on a simply designed accent table, and grouped beside the table were two occasional chairs in chocolate brown.

Iverson laid his briefcase on the large coffee table that stretched from one end of the oversized sofa to the other, and he unsnapped the locks, the loud clicks resounding in the room. He looked at Melissa, who sat down beside him, and he smiled. She reciprocated the gesture, her eyes beaming her confidence and her support.

"As you gentleman know," Iverson began as Melissa picked up the files and handed each of them one, "this is the first joint effort of this kind for me; it's my first step into transportation, and I've invited my father here tonight so that you may clearly understand from the onset that although he and I are in agreement on the feasibility of this proposal, neither he nor his company is financially supporting me, not because he wouldn't, but because I haven't asked him to. This is strictly my project."

Melissa listened as Iverson continued to outline his proposal, and she watched Tom's and George's expressions. But all of the men present were shrewd businessmen and had learned long ago not to show their emotions. Dillson sat in one of the chairs nearest the accent table chewing on his cigar but listening attentively to every word that Iverson said.

Whitman, on the other hand, sat in the bentwood rocker, gently moving to and fro, but he seemed to be preoccupied. He studied the material in the file and seemed to be listening to all that Iverson said, but he didn't interrupt to ask as many questions as Dillson did. Still, Melissa thought as she looked at him, he didn't have to. Just by being quiet and listening, leaving all the inquiring to Dillson, he was learning all he needed to know.

Finally, when he did speak, he addressed Bradley rather than Iverson. "I can't understand why you aren't going into this with Iverson, Bradley."

While Bradley was answering the question Iverson leaned over and whispered to Melissa, "Go into my office and get the cost sheets that are on the top of my desk. I had hoped that I wouldn't need them, but it seems that I do."

Melissa nodded and stood up, quietly slipping out of the room without interrupting the flow of conversation. She raced down the stairs, across the large foyer, into Iverson's office. Without stopping, she flicked on the wall switch, hurrying to the desk. Carefully but hurriedly she thumbed through the stack of papers, looking for the cost sheets. Just as she found them the telephone rang.

Although she instinctively reached for the receiver, she withdrew her hand before she had answered. It wasn't her place to answer it, she thought as she scampered out of the room, leaving the telephone for Estelle. She turned off the light, closing the door behind her, and darted across the foyer to the stairs. She had only climbed two or three steps, however, before Estelle stopped her.

"Ms. Phillips, will you tell Mr. Iverson there's a call for him?"

Smiling at the older woman, Melissa said, "I'm sure Mr. Gerrick wouldn't want to be interrupted right now, Estelle. He's in the middle of a very important business conference. I'll give him a message however, and you go ahead and get the name and phone number. Tell the party that Mr. Gerrick will return the call later."

Estelle pressed her lips together and said, "If it was anybody but Nicole, I would agree, Ms. Phillips. However, Mr. Iverson usually makes an exception for her."

"I see," Melissa replied, not really seeing or understanding. But as Iverson's assistant, it was up to her to make sure he wasn't disturbed. She turned around and headed back toward the office. "Let me see if I can take a message for him."

Estelle shrugged. "That's fine with me. I've got plenty of work to do besides answering telephones and taking messages." Abruptly she turned, gladly retreating behind the closing door.

Again Melissa flicked on the light and walked to the desk, picking up the receiver. "Hello. This is Melissa Phillips. May I help you?"

The silence that followed Melissa's announcement was a short but pronounced one. "I'm sorry," Nicole finally replied in her soft Southern accent, "but I don't think you can. I'm calling Iverson." She was clearly irritated that Melissa had taken the call. "Would you please get him for me?"

"He's in an important conference at the moment and can't be disturbed."

Nicole laughed a low throaty sound that was melodious. "Thank you for telling me. Will you have him call me?"

"I will," Melissa replied. "May I have your name and phone number?"

"I'm Nicole, and he has my phone number." Again Melissa heard that throaty laughter, and she felt as if Nicole were laughing at her. "He knows how to contact me, Ms. Phillips."

"I don't know how long it will be before he can return your call. It may be hours."

"It depends on how quickly you give him the message as to how soon he returns my call. What I'm trying to say," Nicole clarified in stinging tones, "is that Iverson will call me as soon as he gets the message."

That sure of yourself, Melissa spat silently, saying aloud, "I'll give him your message as soon as I can get up the stairs into the study."

"I'm glad you said study, Ms. Phillips," Nicole mocked. "I had wondered in which room the conference was occurring." She laughed, the sound bitter and grating. "Believe me, I know Iverson's tactics. I know all about these evening conferences. He and I have had our share."

57

"Nicole, I assure you, although I don't know why I should bother to, I am only Mr. Gerrick's administrative aide. Our relationship is strictly business. And I also assure you that I shall give Mr. Gerrick your message as soon as I return to the study."

"Then, Ms. Phillips," Nicole replied with a certain smugness, "Iverson will return my call in the next ten or fifteen minutes."

"I can't say."

"How long have you been working for Iverson?" Nicole asked suddenly, burning with an insatiable curiosity, wondering exactly who Melissa Phillips was and what she looked like.

"About a month."

"I see," Nicole murmured faintly. "Evidently not long enough to know about me."

"No."

"But you will," Nicole promised confidently. "That is, Ms. Phillips, if you stay long enough."

"I can't say," Melissa purred sweetly. "Mr. Gerrick doesn't discuss his private life with me, since it's of more interest to him than it is to me. I'm afraid that I would find an account of the women in his life boring." The second of silence that followed her pronouncement was poignant, and Melissa smiled her satisfaction.

"For your sake, Ms. Phillips, you had better give Iverson my message."

"I'll give him the message for his sake, Nicole, not for yours," Melissa returned, gently laying the receiver in the cradle.

Picking up the papers again, she walked out of the room, switching off the light behind her and closing the door. Try as much as she would, though, she couldn't get Nicole out of her mind. She wondered who she was. She wondered what role she played in

58

Iverson's life. The words reverberated in Melissa's mind, haunting her with their sensuality, with their promise. *He has my number! He knows how to contact me!*

"What took you so long?" Iverson demanded under his breath as she sat down beside him, handing him the papers.

"You had a phone call," she whispered. "Estelle had me take it for you."

"Good." He nodded his approval, briefly scanning the column of figures on the papers, absently asking, "Take a message?"

"Um-hm," Melissa informed him. "It was Nicole."

Iverson stiffened, his head jerking up, his eyes glued to Melissa's countenance. "Nicole!" he exclaimed in a husky whisper. "Did she say what she wanted?"

"Said she wanted to talk with you. Asked that you return her call as quickly as possible." She laughed softly. "I told her that it might be hours because you were in . . ." Her words droned into silence as Iverson stood to his feet and walked to the door, calling for Estelle.

Then he spoke to the assembled group. "Gentlemen, I think it's time that we took a break. We've been at it steadily for a couple of hours. How about a cup of Estelle's coffee?"

"Now, that's what I call Southern hospitality," George Dillson sang out. "I'll have several cups. I need some good strong coffee to stimulate my brain."

Iverson smiled vacuously and nodded, his mind clearly on other matters at the moment. "If you need anything, just tell Melissa," he instructed as he walked out of the room. "She'll see to it."

Melissa was infuriated. How dare the man do this to her! She hadn't minded helping him with the dinner; she had wanted to do that. She hadn't even minded when Miss Bromley suggested that they help Estelle cook the meal. She had enjoyed that. But she did resent this! She was not a waitress or a barmaid. She was his administrative assistant; she was his business colleague. And she wanted to be treated like one.

But she hid her anger behind a mask of friendliness, serving the coffee that Estelle brought, guiding the group in polite conversation until Iverson returned, mostly talking with Whitman and Dillson. With Iverson's arrival, discussion quickly reverted to business; however, Melissa noticed that Iverson seemed more tense than he had been before.

Later in the evening George leaned over the coffee table, studying one of the maps that Melissa had prepared for Iverson. "Not bad," he said, rubbing his hand over his chin, his eyes darting from the map to the stat sheet that he held. "This proposal isn't bad at all, Gerrick."

Iverson nodded and turned to Tom. "What do you think?"

"It sounds good," Tom finally admitted, "but there's a lot of risk involved."

"There is," Iverson agreed, "but look at the returns."

"I have been. I just don't know that I'm ready to lay myself open like this. Now, if your father were—"

"But he's not."

Whitman's eyes never left Iverson's face as he slowly nodded his head, and Melissa's eyes never wavered from Whitman's face. "How about Henry Lambert?

"What about him?" Melissa heard the sharp edge in Iverson's question.

"How does he stand?"

"On his feet," Iverson replied, his words firmly planted on granite resolve. "And I stand on mine. This is my baby, Tom. I don't need, nor do I want my ex-father-in-law's endorsement. If I stand, I stand. If I fall, I fall. But it's me. Just me."

Whitman's thin lips moved, but not into a smile. "You're not going to let your bitterness get in the way of your good judgment, are you?" he murmured snidely. "Without Lambert and your father you're liable to fall flat on your butt. And to be perfectly frank, Iverson, I don't relish doing business in that position."

"You must," George hooted gruffly. "You've been doing it that way most of your life." Not letting the soft laughter that echoed through the room stop him, he said, "Personally, I don't know why Lambert should be included. Seems pretty sound to me." He reached up with his stubby hands and took the cigar out of his mouth. "I think, Tom, you're being influenced unduly by another interested party. And I think that certain party is interested only in Lambert Freight International, not in Thomas Whitman or his company." George chuckled softly. "And if you're not careful, you may have reason to be bitter too."

Refraining from making a retort, Iverson suppressed a smile when Whitman glowered his disapproval in Dillson's direction. Quietly he restated his position. "It stands like it is, Tom. Take it or leave it."

Iverson's announcement, like a performance, was followed by the fall of a curtain but no applause. A deep silence fell between him and the others, separating the presenter from the listeners. Finally Whitman nodded, rubbing his long fingers across his chin; Dillson, dropping his cigar stub into an ashtray, leaned over the coffee table and shuffled some papers together; Melissa, walking to the serving cart, lifted the coffeepot and refilled her cup, slowly stirring in the sugar and cream; Orlaine and Bradley silently watched.

"Well"—Iverson eventually spoke, shattering the quiet—"what do you think?" He looked first at Dillson, then at Whitman.

"Frankly," Dillson rasped, "I'm impressed, Iverson. I want to be a part. Not only has it got a future; it *is* the future."

Iverson's lips moved slightly, giving way to a satisfied expression. The russet eyes traveled to the bentwood rocker, and they rested their speculative gaze on Thomas Whitman. "What about you, Tom?"

"I like what I'm hearing, Iverson, but I need more time to think about it. I want to make a thorough study of all your figures." Tom paused, then exclaimed, "Frankly, Iverson, if Henry or Bradley were backing this, there would be no hesitancy on my part to join. But I just don't know." He shook his head, riffling through the stack of papers, pulling out a sheet, looking at the column of figures. "Look at this, for instance . . ."

And with that the meeting continued.

CHAPTER FOUR

Exhausted, Melissa stumbled into the guest bedroom at the Homestead, lethargically changing out of her evening attire into her jeans and shirt. Too tired to do more than repack her cameo brooch, her earrings, and her stole, she curled up in the large round chair that nestled in front of the fireplace, and she baked in the warmth of the glowing flames. Because the meeting had lasted much longer than Iverson had anticipated, he and his father had insisted on Miss Bromley's spending the night, and Iverson had told Melissa that he would drive her home later. Now she waited as he bid his guests good night.

She liked this large room, she decided, not having bothered to put her glasses on, watching the amber shadows dance on the rich wood-paneled walls. It was warm and welcoming. Although the king-size water bed with its brown velvet bedspread was definitely modern, it had been chosen with care and thought, harmonizing with the rustic beauty of this mountain home.

The Iverson Homestead is beautiful, Melissa thought as she slipped in and out of awakeness, trying not to fall asleep. But she was in a dreamlike state where she was unable to distinguish her fantasies from reality. The house wasn't beautiful in a pretty or delicate sense of the word, but it was strong and weathered, she realized. It looked just like Iverson. Or, she thought, maybe Iverson looked just like it.

The knock was so gentle, she wasn't sure that she had heard it. But she sat up, her dreamworld shattered, and she ran her hand through her hair. She looked around, trying to determine what had disturbed her. Then she heard a whisper. She heard the husky vibes of that voice that she had thought so melodious from the onset of their acquaintance. Tonight the gravelly, low-pitched timbre was more than resonant and beautiful; it stirred Melissa's heartstrings, causing her soul to tremble.

"Melissa," he repeated.

She pushed out of the chair, her bare feet whispering across the thick yellow carpet that covered the room. Could that be Iverson? she wondered, never considering that she mentally referred to him by his first name, but always called him Mr. Gerrick to his face.

Again a soft tap and more whispered words. "Are you asleep?"

Melissa, like a forest nymph, glided over the distance that separated them, quietly opening the door, standing back, innocently blinking into that face she had been fantasizing about only seconds ago. She lifted her left hand, raking her hair out of her face, and she smiled tremulously, shaking her head, whispering, "No."

"You're different," he murmured, his eyes glowing a beautiful auburn in the subdued light of the lamp and the fire. Although he had been looking at her clothes, both of them recognized the deeper meaning of his statement.

Her reply was low. "I've just changed clothes."

Iverson's hand came up, and he tenderly whisked her bangs off her forehead, his touch light and caressing. He pulled a silken curl through his fingers and looked at it. Then he shifted his gaze, looking into her face, a lazy smile curving his lips.

For some inexplicable reason neither one of them wanted to play the game of seduction by the rules. Instead of a come-on by him and a coy reply and come-on by her, they both paved the way for truth.

"How did it go?" she asked in a soft voice.

When Iverson lifted his shoulders in a gesture that gave vent to his uncertainty, Melissa nodded her understanding, her eyes running over his wrinkled white shirt with the open collar and the cuffed sleeves, the unbuttoned vest, the tie that was draped around his neck. "You're tired, aren't you?" she asked.

He drew in a deep gulp of air, closed his eyes, and rubbed his hand over them wearily. "Yes, and I'm still not sure where I stand with Whitman." He flexed his shoulders tiredly. "As it is, I can only wait."

Not stopping to consider her actions, Melissa reached out, her fingers gently brushing an errant auburn wave into place. That would have been enough to be considered provocative, but even then she didn't stop. Running her fingertips over his forehead, she traced the furrows of anxiety and worry.

"Why don't you go on to bed?" she suggested with a smile. "There's no need to take me home this late. You're tired, and so am I."

"Don't tempt me," he told her. "I'll probably take you up on it."

"Please do," she pressed. "It won't make that much difference whether I leave tonight or early in the morning with Miss Bromley."

"No plans for tomorrow?"

She nodded. "Plans, but there's plenty of time. I'll just call Mom to let her know not to expect me home tonight, and all's well."

"Okay," he acquiesed willingly, "I'll wait while you call her. If for some reason she should object, I'll drive you home."

"It's not a matter of her objecting." Melissa chuckled, backing out of the way, closing the door behind him. "It's more a matter of courtesy. I'm not asking for permission to spend the night. I'm informing her where I will be so she won't worry unnecessarily." As he walked to the chair that she had just vacated, she moved to the nightstand, lifting the telephone receiver.

In an easy stance, his hands on his hips, Iverson studied her for a long, careful moment, listening as she began to talk with her mother. Then without a word or a gesture he spun on his heel, walking out of the room. Later, when Melissa had concluded her conversation, she walked to the door and stood looking down the large, silent hall. Finally she shrugged and stepped back into the warmth of the room, accepting his unexplained departure.

Just as she was about to close the door, however, she heard his low command. "Don't shut that door. My arms are full."

Her heart lifting with the song of elation, Melissa poked her head around the doorframe, grinning as she watched Iverson slowly move toward her bedroom. With both hands he gripped a large ice chest, and with his chin he balanced on top of it a bag of popcorn, a wire popcorn popper, salt, butter, a big bowl, and a bottle opener. She chuckled when, as he gently set everything on the carpet in front of the fireplace, it toppled to the floor.

"Now," he instructed, without turning to look at her, busily sorting through the goods, "come over here to help me."

Melissa, following his instructions, quietly closed

the door and walked to where he knelt, watching as he poured the popcorn into the popper.

"Ever done this before?" he asked, adjusting the mesh hood on the pot.

"What?" she teased. "Moved into a guy's bedroom lock, stock, and ice chest?"

The rapid jerking of his face in her direction and his scowl were her eye's answer, but the twinkling in the darkness of his eyes was her heart's answer. "Ms. Phillips, I don't need a smartass tonight. I hired you to be that five days a week and more if duty so dictates, but not tonight."

Melissa giggled, once again curling her slight form up in the big chair. "Maybe duty is dictating."

Iverson, still kneeling in front of her, rocked back on his feet. "Don't put the starched uniform back on yet, Melissa. I need a people right now to talk to me." His eyes pleaded with her. "Just a plain ole people."

"I don't know how to take that remark," Melissa retorted. "Plain and old. That, Mr. Gerrick, smirks of an insult if ever I've heard one." Only the laughter in her voice softened her accusation.

"No, Melissa, it's not an insult. It's a compliment of the highest form. Praise truly meant." He opened the ice chest and pulled out two bottles of beer, using a can opener to flip off the caps with a deft twist of the wrist. Handing one of the bottles to Melissa, he lifted the other to his lips and drank, long and deeply. Balancing the popcorn popper over the open flame with one hand, he loosely held the neck of his bottle with the other, dangling that hand over his bent knee.

Then he reflected soberly, "I seldom meet people, Melissa. Very seldom." He looked up into her face, the glow of the fire accenting the craggy ruggedness of his profile and catching the wistful longing in the depth of those mysterious eyes. "You're a refreshing change. I feel as if I can be myself for a change, not the person I have to be in order to impress either this one or that one." He shook the popper, moving it from one side of the flame to the other.

"Thank you, Mr. Gerrick," Melissa murmured, the sincerity of his confession touching the very depth of her soul.

He shook his head, soft laughter rumbling from his hard chest. "Not Mr. Gerrick, Melissa. Call me Iverson."

His smile commanded a returning smile from her, the laughter in his eyes cajoled laughter in hers, and his pursed lips commanded her to say his name.

"Iverson." Whisper soft, the word slipped past her lips to caress his frayed emotions and nerves. "Hello, Iverson." Unaware of the sensuality of her gesture, Melissa leaned downward, holding her hand out to him. "I'm glad to make your acquaintance. I'm Melissa Phillips."

Iverson set down his bottle on the hearth and wiped his hand on the front of his shirt before he caught her small hand in the sinewy grasp of his bigger one. "Hello, Melissa."

He didn't turn her hand loose. He couldn't turn her hand loose. She was real, and right now she belonged to him in his hour of great need. He tugged, pulling her from the chair to sit beside him on the floor in the soft, warm glow of the fire. Without breaking the mood, he handed her the handle to the popper, and he sprinted to his feet, moved across the room, turned off the light switch, and grabbed the pillows from the bed, throwing them on the floor. ·

"Now," he grunted, lowering his large frame beside her, unwrapping the stick of butter and dropping it over the popcorn. "Nobody will disturb us. The light's out, and"—he leaned over and patted the ice chest—

"I don't have to run back to the kitchen for more drinks. We're set for the rest of the night."

Melissa laughed, withdrawing the popcorn from the fire, laying it on the hearth while she got the bowl and salt. "Don't you mean set for the rest of the day? I think we've already passed through the night and have begun a new day."

Iverson grabbed a dishtowel and pulled up the hot hook that held the wire basket together. Then he emptied the popcorn into the bowl. "I think we have begun a new day, Melissa, and I'm glad that you're the one beginning it with me." Holding the bowl in both hands, he leaned against the chair, stuffing the pillow behind himself, throwing a handful of popped corn into his mouth, and munching. "And, since we're beginning this day together, tell me something about yourself."

Melissa stretched out on her stomach, bunching her pillow into a wad, lying her head on it. "No fair. You already know more about me than I know about you. So it's your turn to confess."

"Okay," Iverson returned. "I haven't been to church in a long time, but I feel like confessing tonight. So get comfortable, mother confessor. Here I go."

"Begin, my son," Melissa mimicked. "I hear all."

"Isn't that supposed to be 'forgive all'?" he asked, placing his bottle on the hearth.

Melissa shook her head, their eyes meeting. She realized that he had maneuvered his body so close to hers that their heads were almost touching. "I don't think we'll ever reach the point in our acquaintance that we'll need to forgive all."

"But you never can tell where we may go from here," he contradicted and prophesied in the same breath.

Without touching her he was setting her body on fire; her nerve endings were tingling, and bumps of desire danced all over her soft, creamy skin. His eyes rested on the bed, and he squirmed even closer, his hand brushing against her cheek. He propped himself on an elbow, and he leaned over her, his face coming lower and lower, his breath fanning her cheeks.

"Some people claim I'm just like a compass," she whispered, carefully moving herself, her eyes following his to the bed. "I always know what direction I'm going in, and"—she sat up, pushing away from him, running her hands through her hair—"I'm not headed in the direction of bed. Especially your bed."

"Such a shame. I've been told that I'm really a good lover. And I know for a fact that's a marvelous bed. With such a combination how could you lose?"

Melissa chuckled. "I don't find that hard to believe, Iverson Gerrick. You seem to be good at most anything you do. I shouldn't think you'd be any different in bed."

"Want to find out for sure?" he asked, rolling over.

Again Melissa's rich laughter filled the room. "I'll take your word for it." Then the enormity of his words touched her gently, settling on her heavily, making her too aware of him. She got up and settled into the chair. "Maybe it's time for you to leave, Iverson."

He shook his head. "Let me stay, Melissa. We'll just talk." His eyes pleaded with her eloquently. "I promise, I won't try to push you into anything. I just need company tonight."

"Why?" Melissa asked, knowing that it was more than his concern about Whitman's decision.

Iverson didn't answer immediately; rather, he moved, banking the fire, putting another large log on the low-burning flames. Then he sat down, his back to Melissa, his face to the fire.

"Does it have anything to do with the phone call?" she asked. She hadn't been able to shake the thought of Nicole out of her mind. Push her away temporarily, yes. But she had been unable to get rid of her completely.

She couldn't forget how quickly Iverson had gone running to her, just as Nicole had predicted. He had called as soon as he received her message. Melissa had watched him after he returned, and she thought he seemed preoccupied, as if he had something weighty on his mind, something more than business. And now he was hesitant to answer her.

When Iverson didn't reply, she prompted him. "Does it have anything to do with Nicole's phone call?"

"Did the office grapevine tell you that I'd been married before?" he countered.

"Yes," she whispered, pain constricting her breathing, squeezing all the air out of her lungs. "Nicole." The word slipped past her lips before she was aware that she had thought it.

"Nicole Lambert, from one of the old colonial families of the South. The Lamberts, one of the most distinguished family names on the social register of North Carolina. And owners of one of the most successful corporations in the country." He leaned over, flipped the top of the ice chest off, and delved for another bottle of beer. Opening it, he took a long swig, then murmured, "She's beautiful, Melissa. Nicole is truly beautiful. Everything a man could want in a woman."

"It hardly makes sense," Melissa said stiffly, unable to understand why she was hurting so badly. "If she's all that, why isn't she still your wife?"

"Note," he pointed out bitterly, "I said everything a man could want in a woman, not everything a man

71

wants in a wife. She's the kind of person who's easy to love, Melissa, but she's also the type of person who can't love."

"Yet you married her?"

"I didn't know or understand her at the time," he refuted. "It wasn't until after we married that I learned I was just a possession." Suddenly needing contact with Melissa, he scooted over so that he sat at her feet, his head against her knees, totally unaware of the caressive action. Still staring at the vibrant flames that danced up the chimney, he lifted his beer bottle and took a swallow. "Nicole didn't marry me because she loved me. She married me because I was different, Melissa. I wasn't from her circle of friends or acquaintances. And for a while I greatly amused her. The primitive, untamed mountain man."

"Yet I have the distinct feeling that you love Nicole," Melissa mused.

"No, I don't love her. I recognize that she's a beautiful woman, but I don't love her, Melissa." He shook his head, and Melissa felt his warm flesh through the material of her jeans. Arrows of desire sailed through her body, piercing her heart, alarming her mind. "She enjoyed showing me off. I began to feel like one of those little pomponed poodles on a leash."

Melissa couldn't control her gales of laughter. "Perhaps a German shepherd or a Doberman, but certainly not a little poodle!"

He chuckled softly with her and continued talking. "In the presence of friends and outsiders Nicole was loving and sweet. She made them think I was the center of her life, that we were so happy together. But, dear God, when we got home, it was like a norther had blown in." He suddenly twisted, lifting his head toward her, pleading for understanding. "One can admire an iceberg; one can think it's beautiful, and perhaps one can have a certain type of love for it. But you can't take it in your arms and hold it tight, Melissa. You can't get the warmth you need from it. And that's exactly the way I feel about Nicole. I admire her; I think she's beautiful, but, God only knows, I can't love a woman who's cold and unfeeling, whose only love is herself and her company."

"Her company?"

"She's chairman of the board of Lambert Freight International." He answered her question, going on to say, "She was infatuated with the rough mountain man." His voice lowered. "She never saw me, Melissa. She never saw that I was a person who needed love and warmth. She never understood that I wanted compassion and understanding. I wanted a home and a family. Nicole could see me and marriage only as a sound business deal. She kept pointing out to me that I was getting the endorsement of her father, Henry Lambert, head of Lambert Freight International. What more could I ask for?"

"She didn't want love?"

Iverson again shrugged his massive shoulders. "She wanted sex, but she was rather narcissistic. Her love for herself was enough, and she had no emotion left for me." He leaned forward, setting another empty bottle on the hearth; then he scooted back, squirming into a comfortable position with the side of his face resting against Melissa's leg. "She just liked playing marriage."

"Which one of you tired of playing first?"

"I tired of the game first, but every time I mentioned our getting a divorce, she would change. For a little while she would be sweet and loving. Then I found out that she had a lover, and I wouldn't tolerate that. When I asked for a divorce she begged me to reconsider and promised that it wouldn't happen again. But it did. And I could see the pattern of our marriage developing. I was angry, Melissa. Angry at myself for having loved her and angry because she could manipulate me so easily.

"The second time it happened I didn't reconsider my decision." He paused, remembering. "Perhaps if I had thought she loved me I would have reconsidered, but I couldn't take any more of the hell we were living in. I had no more love to give, and, God help me, I desperately needed love, Melissa. So I divorced her."

Melissa touched him, understanding his desperation, remembering how she felt the night that her mother had announced her decision to get a divorce. She remembered the utter desolation she and her father had felt. She remembered how unprepared they had been.

"I think that Nicole still cares for you," Melissa told him.

"Nicole cares for me only when she thinks I care for someone else or when she thinks someone else cares for me. She doesn't want me, but she doesn't want anyone else to want or to have me either."

"Why did she call tonight?" Melissa asked, knowing that she was letting her curiosity push her beyond the bounds of convention and politeness.

Iverson chuckled, draping an arm over her legs, his fingers running up and down the outseam of Melissa's jeans. "She heard that I had a new woman in my life."

"Me," Melissa whispered on bated breath, wondering who would have told Nicole such a tale like that.

Iverson's chuckle burgeoned into full, deep laughter. "She didn't believe me when I told her that we were in a meeting."

Melissa smiled and chuckled softly. "It must have done her ego wonders when you rushed down to return her call immediately after I had given you the message."

Not answering, Iverson wrapped both arms around her legs and pulled her out of the chair, sprawling on the floor beside her. "Are you jealous, little assistant?" he teased, leaning over her, watching the firelight as it flickered over her face.

"No," she returned, wondering if she was telling the full truth. "I'm not. I was just surprised." She lifted her hand, tracing the outline of his face. "She told me that you would return her call as soon as you received the message, but I didn't think so."

He grinned. "I disappointed you. You thought I was the strong, silent type. The man who took what he needed out of life when he needed or wanted it, totally unconcerned about anyone else's needs or desires."

Melissa nodded her head, unmindful that she was messing up her hairdo. "I guess I did think you were unfeeling."

"I may appear to be unfeeling, but I am not uncaring. I still care about Nicole; I care about what she can do to my company, to my reputation . . . to me." His face lowered, and he whispered, his breath warmly oozing over the sensitive terrain of her face, "My biggest concern was for my meeting tonight. Knowing Nicole like I do, it wouldn't have surprised me for her to have come bursting into the house, disrupting the meeting, destroying all that I had worked for. I couldn't have that. So it was better for her to think that she had pulled me from the arms of my newest lover. It satisfied her warped ego and kept her away from me."

"You let her believe that we are lovers," Melissa murmured, knowing that she should be angry but not really caring at the moment.

"Not only let her believe it," he confessed, "but I told her that we were."

"You lied to her," Melissa exclaimed lightly in a low dreamy voice.

"No," he returned, "I just spoke of things that are to be as if they already were."

"I don't mix business with pleasure," she softly enunciated, her brown eyes flickering gold in the glow of the fire. "I've learned from past experience that the two don't mix."

"Depends on the two people who are mixing them," he returned, his voice mimicking the seductiveness of hers. He lowered his face, his purpose gleaming in his eyes, his mouth hovering over hers. "Let me show you how sweet it can be, Melissa." The honey softness of his request flamed over Melissa.

"No," she whispered, touching his chin with her fingertips, gently pushing it upward, away from her.

"You don't want to?"

"I would be lying if I said I didn't want to," she said, "but it would be wrong for me to let you make love to me now." Her lips, the lipstick long since wiped off, curved into a beautiful, tremulous smile.

"Does that mean that eventually you will?" he asked, his eyes smoldering with a blaze that was burning hotter and brighter than the one in the fireplace.

"I don't think I'll be around that long," she answered.

"What if you are?"

"If I am—then maybe."

"Is that a promise?"

"It's a maybe promise."

Iverson gazed at her longingly for countless seconds before he nodded and stretched his body alongside hers, lying on his back, lifting an arm, bending and crossing it over his forehead. "How binding is a maybe promise, Melissa?"

"More or less," she quipped lightly.

"More or less what?"

"Less binding than a promise but more binding than a maybe."

"Have all your relationships in the past been based on no more than this?"

"I haven't left a string of broken hearts behind, if that's what you're asking. And I haven't been the victim of some terrible heartbreak. Nor have my involvements with the opposite sex been that numerous. On the other hand, I haven't had an undernourished love life either."

"Anything serious?" Iverson asked.

"No," she answered, "nothing serious."

"Why?" he asked, turning and leaning on his side, closing a big hand around her smaller one, gently squeezing it. "Are you afraid of absolutes?"

"No," she answered, closing her eyes, blocking out his hard, rugged visage. "I'm not afraid of absolutes. I just don't know if there is anything absolute in life. And, even if there is, I don't believe that sexual commitments constitute an absolute; I don't think a relationship between a man and a woman should be treated as one."

"Why?" Iverson asked, running his other hand through her hair, pulling the pins out.

"You should know the answer to that one," Melissa countered, suddenly opening her eyes, staring up at him.

"Just because I made a mistake doesn't mean that marriage is an outdated institution or that two people shouldn't promise fidelity to each other. It just proves that we're still human." He rubbed his fingertip around the outline of her face, over the eyebrows, down the nose, across the fullness of her mouth. "What happened to make you feel like this?"

"Life." She shrugged, not wanting to talk, not wanting to destroy the warmth that she felt, wanting this closeness and this togetherness to continue, never to end.

"Some guy hurt you?" he pried.

"No," she answered, turning her head from his compelling and hypnotic touch, "I'm just a product of a shattered absolute. My parents lived together for over twenty years before they divorced. Twenty years they stayed together because of me, not because they loved each other."

"They must have loved each other when they married," Iverson pointed out, hearing a cry of bitterness that came from the depth of her heart.

"No, they didn't love each other. Possibly they cared for each other, but they didn't love each other. When Mom found out she was pregnant, she told Dad, and they agreed that it was for the best if they married, and for the best interest of the child they stayed married."

"Did they have a good marriage?" Iverson asked, his hands continuing to feather-touch her face.

"I thought they did," Melissa returned. "All my life I prided us on having a model family. Other friends' parents were divorcing, but not mine. We were happy, I thought." She suddenly jerked her legs up, levering herself into a sitting position, running from his caressing touch. "Right after I left for the university in Austin, Mom came up here for a visit. When she returned to Galveston, she asked Dad for a divorce."

"Just like that?"

"Just like that," Melissa replied. "While she was here in Asheville, she met Brian Cresswell, and they fell in love. After she and Dad divorced, she returned here to marry Brian."

"What happened to you?" Iverson asked, understanding the sense of loss she felt when her world crumbled from under her.

"I stayed in Austin, burying myself in schoolwork to keep from facing reality, and after I graduated, I returned to Galveston to live and to take care of Dad. I wanted to help him get over the divorce. He was totally wiped out. I guess he'd gotten into the habit of being married and couldn't quite cope without it."

"Why didn't you come to Asheville with your mother?"

"I did come for visits, but Mom didn't need me like Dad did. He had no one, and Mom had Brian. Also, I wanted to stay in Texas at the time, so I stayed and got a job with SeaCo and worked my way from word-processor clerk to office manager in eight years. During that same time I went back to college at night and earned an M.B.A."

"If you enjoyed living in Galveston, what made you decide to leave?"

Melissa turned her head, looking over her shoulder, smiling. "I guess you'll finally get an answer to your question, won't you?"

Iverson scooted closer to her, putting his hands on her shoulders, pulling her back against his chest. Oddly enough, the movement was more comforting than it was sexual. "Only if you want to tell me."

"Brian died," she whispered, compelled to tell him, "and Mom went to pieces, giving up on life altogether. She couldn't believe that after eight short years Brian had been taken away from her. When I came out during my vacation, I couldn't believe the change in her."

"You moved up here because of your mother?" he

questioned softly, his hands moving in deep, massaging motions on her shoulders.

"I suppose I was thinking about moving all along," she admitted. "But I couldn't bring myself to sever the ties. A good job, a beautiful garden home, a car, and Les."

"Les?" Iverson questioned with sharpened interest. "Les, a boy?"

"No," she corrected him, gently shaking her head, "Les Strader, a *man.*" She chuckled when Iverson's hands teasingly dug into her flesh. "On the morning of my twenty-ninth birthday I knew that I had to break out of the rut I was in. I knew that if I was going to make a change, I had to make it now."

"So you quit your job, turned your back on Les, and hightailed it for the mountains."

"Something like that." Melissa smiled, glad that he hadn't wanted her to fill in the details of the picture.

Cuddled together, snuggled up on the carpet in front of the fire, they sat watching the glowing red-orange flames as they lapped up the walls of the chimney, skipping and hopping over the burning logs. They lapsed into a comfortable quietness, content to sit. Finally, however, the tiredness of the day overcame both of them.

Melissa's golden-brown eyes were innocent and dreamy. "I think it's time that we went to bed."

"I agree."

"Not together. You, in your bed. Me, in this one."

"How much better if we were to sleep in the same one," he returned, stretching out on the carpet, pulling her close to him. "How much more fulfilling."

"No," she said, rolling out of his arms, jumping to her feet. "And it's time for you to go fill your bed, and I'll fill mine."

80

"How about a good night kiss?" he murmured, laughter glinting in the depth of those auburn recesses.

"I'll consider a good night kiss once you've cleaned up this mess and are on your way out of my room."

"Yes, ma'am," he snapped, hopping around, gathering the empty bottles, dropping them into the ice chest. Then he picked up all the popcorn paraphernalia, stuffing it into the bowl. "All done," he announced, looking quite pleased with himself. "Now for my good night kiss." He reached for her.

"Oh, no," she told him, dancing away from him. "Let's move this"—she tapped the ice chest and the bowl with her toes—"out of my room."

"Into my room," Iverson suggested, grinning wickedly.

"Into the kitchen," Melissa countered dryly. "I'm not about to jump out of the frying pan into the fire."

"God! Melissa," he cried with deep feeling, "I wish you would. I have a feeling that sharing fire with you would be more wonderful than words can describe." His eyes slowly traveled over the delicate features of her face, the big eyes, the spreading of freckles, the turned-up nose, the golden-brown bangs that fringed her forehead. His hands reached for her again, and this time, mesmerized by his eyes, spellbound by the low, hypnotic vibes, Melissa moved closer to him. "Please jump," he whispered, his body begging for her sweet touch.

"I can't."

"Why?" he breathed, drawing her to himself, the strong arms closing around her body, the sensuous lips moving in a straight line for her mouth. "Afraid of the fire or of falling?"

"Yes," she answered vaguely, lifting her arms, wrapping them around his back, her fingers kneading his taut, flexed muscles.

"There's nothing to be afraid of."

"I know," she whispered, "but I don't have a parachute on, and I'm afraid of falling—" She hadn't planned on being so honest, but she felt comfortable enough to share her fears with him.

"Afraid of falling in love?" He sighed, his lips lightly touching hers, sending exquisite splinters of delight sparking through her.

"More afraid of falling too fast," she replied, no longer resisting the ecstasy that his nearness brought. She successfully blocked out all her doubts, her fears, her inhibitions.

"Don't be afraid. I'm here to catch you. I won't let anything hurt you, darling."

"Not intentionally," she agreed.

"We can have a gorgeous love."

"I'm not afraid of love," she confessed, and paused, her arms tightening around him as she felt a shudder of passion rack his body. "I'm terrified of lust, and I'm not sure what the line of difference is."

"Have you ever been in love before?" he questioned, nuzzling her cheek, burrowing his face in the sweet-scented skin under and behind her ear, his tongue flicking, igniting all the numerous nerve endings that weren't already burning.

"Never," she returned, her hands acquainting themselves with the firm muscularity of his back, moving down the crevice of his spine, feeling the incline of flexed muscle on either side. She shivered as she felt his arms encircle her, hard as iron yet tender as a baby's touch.

"Truly this is a new day for both of us," he whispered.

"Iverson," Melissa mumbled as she tried desperately to surface to reality. "I—I—" He wouldn't stop his caressing; his lips and his tongue explored the vulnerability of her face, her lips, her neck, and her ears. "I don't want to be consumed by lust, and I'm not looking for love." She mumbled incoherently, "I don't want to want you."

"Baby, baby," he implored, with a soft laugh, "I don't think it's a matter of what you want anymore; I think it's out of our hands. Whether we wanted to or not, we have unwittingly started walking the path of love."

"Or lust," she whispered, his lips covering hers, silencing further talk and silencing denials.

His arms tightened around her slight form, and he lifted her off her feet, arching himself, pressing her to the firm arousal of his body. His tongue softly wisped across her mouth, seeking entrance into its forbidden depths. Yet she clenched her teeth together, denying him access to her susceptibility.

"No, baby," he gritted, barely lifting his mouth from hers. "This won't do." With a fluid motion he gathered her into his arms and carried her to the water bed, both of them sailing through the air to tumble gently into the watery mattress. "You promised me a good night kiss, and I want a kiss."

"Iverson," Melissa pleaded, "please, don't."

But he wouldn't be stopped. His hands slipped under her blouse, up the creamy expanse of her midriff to cup the tender breasts that were covered by a wisp of lace. "Yes, Melissa," he breathed, cradling his face in the curve of her neck and shoulder. His lips ravaged her, and his tongue burned designs into her skin.

Her frame shuddered, and she gasped as she felt her breasts tighten and throb under the caress of his fingertips. Taking advantage of her moan of ecstasy, Iverson shifted his weight and lifted his face, his lips touching her opened ones, his tongue quickly, deftly, moving into the moist warmth of her mouth.

83

His lips tenderly explored hers, nipping them and whetting her desires, stirring her senses. But still the caress didn't deepen into a reciprocal kiss, and Iverson demanded this. He didn't want just sex; he wanted her warm softness and her caring. More than anything, he needed someone to care about him. His arms folded around her as he tumbled to his side, gathering her close to his chest and stomach.

"Kiss me, Melissa," he demanded, never moving his mouth from hers. "Kiss me, darling."

Pushing all inhibitions aside, Melissa placed one of her hands on his shoulder, and, at the same time that she pushed herself upward, she shoved him on his back. Leaning over him, her hair falling around her face, she whispered, "I'm going to kiss you good night, Iverson." Her hand feathered across his cheek, rasping across the sandpaper beard that stubbled his face. "But that's all."

"Maybe not," he whispered, bringing his hands up to cup her face. "I hope not. I hope it's just the beginning."

"It may be a beginning," she confessed softly, "but this is all for tonight." Her lips, like the gentle brush of butterfly wings, touched his.

"How can you say that, baby?" he moaned, his hands flowing up and down her back. "You've got to be as hungry for a taste of me as I am for you."

"I'm not just hungry. I'm starved. But I'm going to assuage my hunger slowly. I'm going to be very cautious where you're concerned, Iverson Gerrick." Very cautious, she silently added, letting her lips seal her promise with one last kiss.

CHAPTER FIVE

When Melissa felt the gentle ripple of the water mattress, she stretched her legs and breathed deeply, but she didn't awaken. Rather, she buried her face in the thick softness of the down pillow and squirmed into a comfortable ball again. But when she felt the warmth immediately beside her, she roused, and when she felt the body that slowly molded its masculine form to her curves, she was instantly alert. She tried to turn over, but she was tightly wrapped in the bedspread and sheet, an arm and a leg binding her. She began to wiggle, trying to free herself.

"Hey!" Iverson chuckled. "No cause for alarm. It's only me."

"I've figured that much out," she panted, finally getting one arm out from under the cover. "What are you doing in here?" Her free arm was wildly thrashing around the nightstand area as she fumbled for her glasses.

"I wish that what I'm really doing here and what I would like to be doing here were the same," Iverson softly said, reaching across her slight form to pick up her glasses and hand them to her. "I thought maybe you would like to have breakfast with me."

He moved, and Melissa, fully awake, emerged from her warm cocoon. She propped herself up on both elbows and pushed her glasses over her nose, staring at him incredulously. "Breakfast!" she grimaced. "Who wants breakfast? I want my sleep." Abruptly she changed the subject, asking, "What time is it anyway?" Without waiting for an answer, she peered around one of his massive shoulders, sputtering, "It's still dark outside. Why aren't you in bed?"

Iverson grinned, shifting to a sitting position. "Because I'm afraid of the dark and because I don't like sleeping by myself. Furthermore," he added, unbuttoning his shirt, "you hadn't given me the invitation. But it won't take me long. Here, let me take my clothes off."

Melissa shook her head and laughed. "Iverson, have you even gone to bed?"

He nodded, his fingers stopping their task, the white shirt partially unbuttoned. His somber gaze touched her heart. "I went to bed, but I couldn't sleep. I kept thinking about you, and—" He never completed his sentence. He just smiled at her, the light from the fire flickering shadows across his face.

"You built a fire," she stated simply.

"I didn't want you to get chilly while you were dressing." His eyes lighted on her shoulders that contrasted pearly-white against the dark brown of the quilted spread.

"You—" Melissa cleared her throat, hoping to swallow the nervousness that his gaze generated, wishing she could quell the churning in her stomach. "You wanted me to eat breakfast with you?" He nodded. "Where?"

"I could cook it, and we could eat it here in bed," he suggested lightly. "Afterward we could have dessert."

Melissa grinned. "I never have dessert with breakfast."

"Such a shame," Iverson told her, stretching across the bed, his shirt falling open to reveal his broad, smooth chest, the red-orange shadows playing across the flexed muscles. "You've been missing out on so much in life."

Melissa grinned. "And you, Mr. Gerrick, would like to come to my rescue and introduce me to all the wonders that I've been missing."

Iverson chuckled, the raspy sound infectious. "Although a backwoodsman and a mountain man, Ms. Phillips, I have acquired all the charm and culture of the Southern cavalier. I would count it an honor and a privilege to introduce you to these wonders."

Said in jest, Iverson meant his words, and Melissa knew it. While they stared at each other in silence, his hand slowly pulled down the cover, letting it slide, baring her shoulders. He saw the gentle slope of her breasts that enticingly peeped above the lacy line of her bra for just a moment before she grabbed the blanket and covered herself. Because she hadn't planned to spend the night, she hadn't brought a nightgown and had gone to sleep in her underwear.

"If—if ever I should need a champion, Mr. Gerrick," she said, her eyes never leaving the rugged contours of his face that were outlined and shaded by the dancing firelight, "I will certainly consider your offer."

"Until then, Melissa, will you join me for the day. We'll do whatever you want, starting with breakfast at Mount Haven Inn."

"I would love to," she told him regretfully, "but I've already made plans." She tried to pull the cover up higher, but Iverson's hand curved over hers and stopped all movement.

"Melissa, please spend the day with me." She heard the little boy in him calling out. She heard the loneliness; she heard the desperation.

Then in a most disarming gesture, Iverson laid his

head against her breast and put his arms around her. It wasn't meant to be sensual; rather, it was an innocent gesture that mirrored his loneliness. Unplanned, unrehearsed, it was the most devastating tactic the man could have used, and Melissa responded to him from the very bottom of her soul. She wrapped her arms around him and held him, giving of herself unselfishly, giving him her strength.

"Iverson," she whispered, comforting him, rubbing her hands through his hair as her mother had done so many times when she was a little girl in need of consoling, "what's wrong? Why are you doing this to me?"

He lifted his head and he broodingly stared into her eyes. "I don't know. I honest-to-God don't know. What's even more shattering, Melissa, is that I don't know what you're doing to me." His fingers gently read her face, not missing a detail, flowing over the satiny surface. "I used to have my life under control. Knew what I wanted. Knew where I was going. Nobody was going to stop me. Nothing was going to come between me and my work."

Melissa's body sang with the implication of his confession, and she pouted her lips, softly kissing the tip of his finger that rested there. "Am I a nobody?"

"You were a month ago, but you're not now," he admitted honestly, his eyes moving across her face. His finger traced her lips, caressing their fullness, outlining them, setting Melissa on fire with desire. "How do I affect you?"

"You're getting me so mixed up, I'm not sure."

"Is it good or bad?" he asked, his voice barely carrying above the spitting and sputtering of the fire.

"It—it feels good, but I don't know if it'll be good for us or not."

He dropped his head against her breast, and he

moved even closer to her body, drawing her into his hard, uncompromising lines. "I told you it would be good for us, Melissa. And it will." His mouth nipped her breast above her bra line, tasting the warmth of her skin, feeling the strength that flowed through her small form.

Melissa's breathing was heavy, and she unconsciously moved her back, slightly arching it, her body automatically reaching out for his sweet touch. Her needs surfaced, meeting and matching his. She reached out emotionally for the man who seemed so vulnerable in her arms.

"If—if you were to ask me," she whispered, "I don't think I could turn you down."

The quietness stretched into silence, but it wasn't uncomfortable or heavy. It was peaceful and serene; it was warm and all-encompassing. She had offered him her gift, the most wonderful gift she could give him— her caring, her wanting to share his need with him.

He lifted his head. "I don't think," he said, raising a hand to gently push stray hairs away from her face, "I can ask you now." Her eyes articulated the question that she couldn't voice. "I would like to make love to you, Melissa, but I don't dare do it now. This is the time for me to take the strength that you offer, for me to take the care that you extend to me, but it's not the time for me to take your physical love." Melissa's lips curled upward at the corners into a glorious smile. "We need to explore our emotions together a little longer. We need to build our caring before we begin our sharing."

Happily she tightened her arms around him, hugging him. "I'm so happy, Iverson, that I could easily scale the highest mountain in the world. I believe I could climb Mt. Everest, but I'll settle for Mt. Pisgah."

Iverson rolled on his back and chuckled at her exuberance. "That's not the kind of exploring I had in mind."

"You said we'd do anything that I wanted to do, and I want to climb a mountain."

"So be it," Iverson announced, putting an end to all discussion. "If you can cancel your other plans, it'll be great. Get dressed and we'll slip out of the house before anyone is up to stop us."

Melissa nodded, but she didn't move. "Are you sure this inn is going to be open this early?"

"I'm sure," he said, getting off the bed and walking to the door. "I'll be back in a few minutes. I'm going to tell Miss Bromley that I'm taking you home, and you can call whomever you have to."

"You can tell Miss Bromley that you're taking me home, but I don't dare call whomever at this time of the morning," Melissa told him. She could just envision waking Penny up this early! "I'll call later on in the day. Whomever would never forgive me."

Iverson turned the doorknob, but he didn't immediately open the door. "Is whomever a man?"

"Yes," she returned impishly, unable to resist the teasing gibe, withholding her little secret just a little longer. It filled her with a small sense of power to know that this powerful man, seemingly hewn out of rock, could be affected by someone like her. "Quite handsome, matter of fact."

"You haven't known him very long, have you?"

"Longer than I've known you," she returned.

This time the silence was almost unbearable. Finally, however, Iverson asked, his voice subdued, "Are you going with me today because you think you have to, because you want Day's Work to have my stamp of approval?"

"I'm going because I want to."

90

"I just wondered if you were breaking a date that you'd rather keep because I've put you in an embarrassing position that you can't extricate yourself from."

"I have the genius and talent of Houdini," Melissa quipped, touched to see this tender side of him. Her voice softened. "I never get caught in predicaments unless I want to be caught." He nodded, his hand turning the doorknob. She knew that she couldn't let him leave the room without telling him the truth. "I was going to let my two nephews take me on a tour of the Biltmore House and Gardens."

There was no smile on his face, but Melissa could see the relief that slowly fused through his powerful body. "Thanks." He sighed, leaving the room, softly closing the door behind himself.

Melissa scurried across the carpet into the bathroom, quickly taking off her underwear and showering. She thought she heard the telephone ringing, but with the water running she couldn't be sure. Then she dismissed the idea as preposterous. Who would call this early in the morning?

Quickly she dried off and redressed, combing her hair and brushing her teeth. Glancing at the clock, she decided to call her mother and ask her to call Penny later and explain that she couldn't make it. She walked across the room and picked up the receiver, holding it to her ear before she dialed.

She heard a feminine voice, and she recognized it as Nicole's. Quickly, after only overhearing a word or two, she jerked the phone away from her ear as if it were a hot coal and hung it up. The telephone *had* rung, she thought, and it hadn't been her imagination. What did Nicole want this early in the morning? Thinking about all this, she packed her suitcase. When she was done, she picked up the phone and called her mother. She then sat down in front of the fire in the big chair, tying her tennis shoes when Iverson knocked on the door.

"The door's open. Come on in."

"I can't," he told her, "or I would."

Melissa went to the door and opened it, her eyes landing on the tray. "You fixed us some coffee," she exclaimed, breathing deeply of the steaming aroma. "And you've changed your clothes."

Her eyes appreciatively ran over his length, and she openly admired the jeans that flattered the muscular legs, that accented his lean athletic physique—the narrow hips, the trim waist. She admired the broad shoulders that tightly stretched the material of his pullover sweater. This was the first time she had seen him in casual clothes, and she liked what she saw.

"Yes, to both counts," he retorted, setting the tray on the small table between the chairs in front of the fire. "I thought maybe you'd like to have one for the road."

"I would," Melissa replied, lifting the coffeepot and pouring the two cups full. Quickly she added sugar and cream to hers, stirring, greedily drinking that first deep gulp. She swallowed, glowing in Iverson's direction. "Mr. Gerrick, last night you proved that you were an excellent businessman, and this morning you've proven that you're a wonderful host. You think of everything."

Iverson lifted the rim of his cup to his lips, holding it there, lapsing into an introspective silence rather than retorting. Finally he said, "I try to think of everything, Melissa, and I try to be an excellent businessman. But sometimes that isn't enough."

"Worried?" she asked, wondering if his mind was on the project or on Nicole.

"Concerned."

"The project?" When he nodded, she said, "It's very important to you, isn't it?"

"This is one of the most important projects I've created, and it's the most important deal that I've ever negotiated." He turned his head and looked at her face in the dim light of the fire. "I would do anything to get this deal through, Melissa. Anything."

"Those are mighty strong words," she said, tiny alarms ringing in her ears, setting her nerves tingling. "There's no end to *anything*, no boundary whatsoever."

"But I mean it," he asserted in a deathly quiet voice. "I learned long ago that in order to get what I wanted out of life I must be prepared to pay the cost. Therefore, I never undertake any plan of action until I've examined all the options and all the possible consequences. I never negotiate a deal unless I've counted the total cost!"

"Why is this so important?"

Stretching his legs, warming his feet close to the roaring blaze, he explained, "This is my first endeavor as Iverson Gerrick, independent of Dad's company. It's mine," he affirmed. "All mine."

Melissa made no reply, but she shivered with apprehension. She was hearing the hard, unfeeling executive, Iverson Gerrick, speak. He was so different from the man who had held her close less than an hour ago. She wondered if she had made a mistake agreeing to spend the day with him; she wondered if he would revert back permanently to the cold, indomitable man with whom she had been working for the past month.

He took several gulps of coffee and stared pensively at the jumping flames, alone in a world that seemed to totally exclude Melissa. Then he turned his head and caught her staring at him. He smiled slowly, reaching across the table to take her hand in his. Again the

93

tenderness of the gesture disarmed her, dissipating her apprehensions and doubts.

"Today is your day, missy, and we're not going to mess it up with business. I've got a special treat in store for you. You want to climb your mountain, and so you shall. Nothing"—he paused, then said more firmly—"nothing is going to spoil it."

Melissa couldn't shake the heaviness that seemed to hover above them like a black cloud. Quietly sipping her coffee, she tried to push the feeling aside, but she couldn't. She wished that it were something they could talk about, but at this point in their involvement she couldn't force him to tell her what had happened to change his mood. Finally, however, Iverson seemed to break away from his pensiveness and began to talk, charming her with stories about mountain climbing, and she forgot her earlier fears and apprehensions.

After another cup of coffee they tiptoed out of the house, laughing like children. Then in the breathtaking beauty of the morning, Iverson drove on the narrow backroads, headed for the small, rustic mountain inn. Melissa, looking out the window, viewed the sun as it began its majestic climb in the sky, and she saw the peaks of the mountains appear in the early morning mist.

"What's the inn like?" she asked excitedly, her eyes glowing and her face shining with anticipation.

"Just an old farmhouse that's been turned into a restaurant and an inn. The Barkers, who run it, converted it about ten years ago."

"Isn't it a big tourist attraction?" Melissa asked, disappointment dulling her excitement. She had hoped they were headed somewhere romantic and secluded.

"It's got quite a reputation," Iverson explained, "but it hasn't been ruined by commercialization. The cabins are built off from the house and blend into the

94

countryside. The house itself is the original restaurant and has several grand suites for special guests. And it's situated right on Lake Peaceful."

"Good fishing?" Melissa inquired, her interest returning.

"Some of the best in North Carolina."

"Trout?" She could just see herself with her rod, reeling in one of those gorgeous creatures.

Iverson laughed. "Trout. Are you a fisherman?"

"I am," she admitted proudly. "That's what comes of being an only child with a father who loves hunting and fishing. You have no choice but to be a sportsman."

"If I had known that, Melissa Phillips, I would have brought some fishing tackle and would have taken you fishing. I never thought to ask. I just took it for granted that you wouldn't. Nicole didn't."

Melissa forced her reply to be light. "Just remember for future reference, I'm not Nicole."

"Point well taken." He grinned at her.

"Next time we'll go fishing," she automatically promised, never considering that there wouldn't be a next time, adding, "I remember one time when Dad and I went fishing. We caught . . ."

And then as Iverson turned off the blacktop and headed down an even narrower mountain road, they swapped fish tales, seeing who could outdo the other. Finally Iverson, driving past the large lake, pulled the car up in front of a gray, weathered two-story house that was completely surrounded by a large veranda and was nestled in the side of the mountain.

"Oh, Iverson!" Melissa gasped when she realized where they were. "This is glorious."

Iverson stopped the car, and she jumped out, looking in all directions, scanning the distance. The lake was beautiful, the water clear and blue, stretching out for miles. She could see the mountain stream that turned into a waterfall before it fed into the lake.

By this time he was beside her, cupping her elbow with his hand. He led her inside the building, choosing a table that was close to the black, pot-bellied stove at the side of the room. As soon as they were seated at the table, an elderly woman with twinkling gray eyes and snow-white hair that was swept in gentle waves from her face to a knot on the top of her head walked into the room, carrying an old-fashioned coffeepot. Over her cotton dress she wore a large apron in a small country print. Briskly she walked to their table, turning Iverson's cup right side up, pouring his coffee.

"Good morning, Mr. Iverson." Her smile was bright and welcoming. "Been expecting you. Got your breakfast ready and your lunch packed." She turned her face to Melissa, cordially including her in the warm greeting, asking, "Would you like to have some coffee, miss?"

"Please," Melissa replied.

"Miss Mary Jane," Iverson said, "I'd like you to meet a friend of mine, Melissa Phillips."

"Glad to meet you, Miss Melissa." Mary Jane's gray eyes twinkled with life and energy. "Glad you could come down with Mr. Iverson. I'm sure that you'll enjoy your stay. There's nothing as good for the soul or the body as the likes of these here mountains."

Iverson grinned and winked at Melissa. "Miss Mary Jane hasn't been out of these mountains for the past fifty years, have you?"

"No, sir, not for any length of time, I haven't," she said, looking down at him, grinning. "And if I have any say-so about it, I won't be a-going. Now, what'll you have this morning?"

"Whatcha got?"

"Eggs and country ham. Grits and home-churned butter. Biscuits and mountain sourwood honey."

"I'll take it all in double portions." Iverson laughed. "One for me, and since I don't know your eating habits as of yet"—he winked at Melissa—"I'll let you order your own."

Without any hesitation Melissa ordered. "It sounds so delicious that I want everything you just listed, and"—she grinned, golden spirals of amusement twirling through her eyes—"I'm only going to take singles, but if that should prove not to be enough, may I have seconds?"

Mary Jane threw her head back and laughed with genuine amusement, immediately liking this new girl Mr. Iverson had brought with him. So many that came she didn't like. But this one . . . Well, she was different. She reminded her of this mountain, pure and innocent, not affected by conventions and false traditions.

"There's plenty more where the firsts'll come from," Mary Jane promised as she walked away. "I'll see that you get enough. Furthermore, I've packed you the best picnic lunch you've ever seen. If the breakfast ain't enough, little lady, you'll have a feast for lunch."

"What does she mean?" Melissa asked when Mary Jane disappeared behind a closing door.

"You wanted to climb a mountain," Iverson reminded her, "and while I don't mind mountain climbing, it's not my favorite sport. So I decided that instead of climbing Mt. Pisgah, we'd climb Mt. Haven, since it's a lot smaller. So I called Miss Mary Jane, telling her that we were coming and what we planned to do." The russet eyes glowed. "She planned the rest. Okay with you?"

"Fine," Melissa replied.

When Mary Jane returned later with their break-

97

fasts, she spoke as she set their plates in front of them. "I like your new young lady, Mr. Iverson. I'm mighty glad to see you with her instead of with Miss Nicole." She added over her shoulder as she walked away, "I never did like that woman."

Again the mention of Nicole's name sent shivers running down Melissa's spine, and she glanced furtively at Iverson. She saw his features tighten, but he made no comment. Rather, he picked up his cup, walked to the woodstove, and lifted the coffeepot, refilling his cup. Before setting the pot on the burner, he held it in her direction. "Want another cup?"

"No, thanks," she replied, again wishing that she could question him, but knowing she had no right to pry.

After breakfast Mary Jane brought them a huge basket filled with food, and set it on their table. Then the two of them walked out of the inn with the basket, standing quietly on the porch for a long time before Iverson caught her hand in his and tugged gently. "Come with me. I want to show you something special." He led her down the steps to the back of the building straight to a path that ran into the dense lush forest.

Mary Jane, standing in the kitchen, looking out the window, spied the young couple, and she smiled as she watched them walk down the pathway that was canopied with the graceful white-laced bows of the dogwoods. They reminded her of a couple walking down the aisle of nature's cathedral. Not a matchmaker, but a romantic at heart, Mary Jane could only hope that one day Iverson would find happiness with someone like Melissa.

She seemed to be good for him, Mary Jane decided. He was more relaxed than she had seen him in a long time. And he was smiling. Maybe Melissa could make him happy. Mary Jane certainly hoped so. She couldn't remember when the last time was that she had seen Iverson happy and carefree. Nor, she thought, turning from the window, placing the plates in the dishwasher, had she ever seen Iverson take any other women to the Haven of Rest. Maybe, just maybe, this one was going to be different.

Farther and farther into the thickness of the forest Iverson and Melissa walked, until they came to a clearing and to a small white frame church. Melissa almost held her breath in awe. She couldn't believe the beauty of the simple building, peacefully cloistered among the gigantic trees, and haloed by the pristine whiteness of the surrounding dogwoods that were in full bloom.

"The Haven of Rest," Iverson murmured softly. "This church was the first structure to be built once the pioneers had reached the valley where they intended to settle. The mountain they called Mt. Haven, and the church they named Haven of Rest."

Melissa stopped at the small fence that encircled a family cemetery. Opening the wrought iron gate, she followed the well-kept path through the graves, reading the headstones. All were Iversons. She turned. "Does all this property belong to you?"

"It belonged to my mother, and on her death we inherited it."

"Is one of these graves hers?" Melissa inquired.

Iverson again nodded. "Elizabeth Anne Iverson Gerrick." He shoved away from the tree and moved inside the wrought iron fence. "She was married here, she lived here, and she died here. She was a wonderful woman, Melissa. Strong and brave but soft and feminine. She gave meaning to our lives."

"Who all does the *our* include?" Melissa questioned, edging closer to him, catching his hand in hers.

"I have a brother and a sister."

"Older or younger?"

"In our family," he told her with a grin, "you can always tell the oldest son because he bears the name Iverson. Customarily the Iverson women honor their oldest sons with this name, their children keeping the tradition alive."

"Does that mean that your son will be named—" Melissa's face jerked up to his and her eyes widened as an unsavory thought flashed through her mind. Perhaps there was already an older son. "You and Nicole"—the question came out almost like a plea— "you didn't have any children?"

"No children," he returned. "That didn't work into her scheme of things. She didn't have time for pregnancy or parenting."

Abruptly Iverson changed the subject and began to tell her about his ancestors, guiding her to a small log building that was close to the church. They left their lunch basket here and dangled their bottle of wine by a cord into the nearby icy stream. Then they whiled away the hours, climbing the mountain, finally reaching the summit. Here they stood, looking at the magnificent panorama of Lake Peaceful.

"Oh, Iverson," Melissa cried, her breath coming in short gasps, "this is the most beautiful view I've ever seen. It's gorgeous."

"But not quite all that you're going to see," he told her, draping an arm over her shoulder, gently turning her in another direction. Pointing to a swinging bridge, he asked, "Are you up to walking from Iverson's Point to Gerrick's Peak?"

Melissa clapped her hands like a child, her eyes wide and glowing. "The Iversons owned one half of the mountain and the Gerricks the other?" she guessed.

100

"You got it."

"And they fussed and fought about it," she continued excitedly.

"Sorta."

"An old family feud?"

Laughing, he shook his head. "Sorry, one or two disagreements, but no family feuds."

"Oh," Melissa drawled, disappointed. "I thought you were really a mountain man."

"I'm sorry," he apologized lightly. "Does it make a difference in the way you feel about me?"

"Well," she droned, pretending to think about it. "Yes, it does make a difference."

"Could I redeem myself if I told you that although the two families didn't feud, the Iversons and Gerricks were moonshiners and bootleggers?"

"Moonshiners and bootleggers!" she exclaimed. "How exciting! That's even better!" She laughed, catching his hand in hers. "You are redeemed, Mr. Gerrick, totally and absolutely redeemed as long as you promise to tell me all about it."

Again hand in hand, they neared the edge of the peak, stepping on the bridge that swayed in the strong mountain breeze. They walked to the middle and stopped, the wind whipping Melissa's hair around her face, lifting the collar of her shirt and flattening it against her neck and cheeks. Unclasping her hand, Iverson laid an arm across her shoulder, and she stood in the comforting circle. She lifted her face, smelling the briskness of spring, smelling the sheer masculinity of the man who stood next to her.

Sensing her awareness of him, Iverson slowly turned her body so that they were completely facing each other, and were oblivious to their precarious position. His lips sought hers, finding them, their warmth and solace. His firm mouth, chilled by the wind, softly touched hers, moving, begging for a reciprocation of his desires.

"Melissa," he uttered in between butterfly strokes on her lips, her cheeks, her neck, her ears, "you taste so good. You feel so good to me. I just wish we could stay up here forever, far above the world."

"Our little hideaway," she said, sighing as she wound her arms around his neck, holding on to him as the bridge swayed slightly in the wind, her lips pecking messages of desire all over his face.

Then a large gust of wind came, and both of them staggered against the cord railing, grabbing the lines with both hands. Laughing, they retraced their steps, following the path down the mountain, moving past the stream, past the waterfalls, back to the church. Here in the warmth of the early afternoon they sat on two large boulders.

Suddenly inspired, they slipped their shoes off, and holding them in hand, waded and splashed in the cold water until they were chilled. Then they sought a warm spot in the sun so they could dry out. Tossing their shoes in one direction, they lay down on their backs, holding hands, their eyes closed, lazing in the golden warmth of the sun, each lost in the realm of thought.

Melissa didn't know how to reckon with this changed Iverson. She had found it easy to hate the executive, to keep her distance. But this vulnerable man was certainly making a place for himself in her heart. Already he was a threat to her peace of mind. Already he was a part of her most private thoughts, and he could so easily become a part of her intimate self. It was so frightening that she shivered.

"Are you still cold?" Iverson asked, rolling over on his side, throwing his arm and leg over her, pulling her closer to his body.

"Not really," she answered. "Just thinking." *Just wondering,* she wished she could say. *Just wondering what an affair with you will be like. Just wondering if we could get past Nicole to have an affair.*

He jumped to his feet, caught her hands in his, pulling her up. "Come on. I've got a wonderful idea. Let's go get our basket. It's lunchtime. In fact, my stomach says it's past lunchtime."

Together, arm in arm this time, they leisurely ambled to the small log house to get their lunch basket. Then they walked to the stream where they had left their bottle of wine. Kneeling on a small boulder, Iverson pulled on the cord.

"Ummm," he ventured, his hands closing around the bottle, "it feels just right. I can tell that we're gonna have a scrumptious lunch."

Melissa took the tablecloth out of the basket and laid it on a large flat boulder, spreading the food on top of it. "Good gracious, Iverson, look what Mary Jane packed for us. We'll never get through it all."

Then all talk ceased, and they quickly ate their lunch. Afterward they cleaned up the clutter and sat back to finish their wine, again enjoying the beauty of the warm spring day, enjoying the presence of each other. They talked a bit, then they lapsed into moments of quietness. Yet they were together. In one of their quiet moments Iverson leaned forward, setting his glass down. The movement, though slight, caught Melissa's attention, and she looked at him.

Never in her life had she felt as she did this very minute. She felt as if she had lost herself in him—as if she had left the world somewhere far behind. She stood on the mountain of her secret dreams, the wind caressing her as it blew all trouble and despair away. She saw only Iverson; she saw only those beautiful russet eyes that flickered enigmatically. When he cap-

103

tured her hand in his, she felt his strength, and she knew that she would walk beside him no matter where their love may take them.

Her heart began to beat erratically, and her blood soared through her veins as she saw the question in his eyes. Uttering no words, she unleashed her desire, letting it run rampant through her body, letting it glaze her eyes, shading them dark and vibrant.

Without a word, barely moving, he released her hand, took the half-empty glass from her unresisting fingers, and set it aside. Next he reached toward her face and gently, as if he were caressing her, as if he were already loving her, he removed her glasses and laid them on the picnic basket. He moved again, his hands closing around her shoulders, and he gently pressed her into the soft lushness of the grass with the weight of his body. Melissa smiled tentatively, lifting a hand to touch his tousled auburn hair that outlined the craggy visage hovering so near hers. His eyes clearly defined his purpose, but she didn't mind. Her purpose was the same; therefore, she welcomed his weight and invited his touch.

"I must know you, Melissa," he beseeched her, his face dropping to the curve of her throat and shoulder. "I must know you better."

"Have we been together long enough for this?" she countered tremulously on stifled breath.

"We've known each other forever." His voice was raspy and thick, and his lips traveled over the arched center column of her neck, up her chin, around the planes of her face.

"That should be long enough, don't you think?"

"I should think," he breathed, setting his mouth on top of hers, tasting her words, the succulence of her lips.

Her arms slipped around his shoulders, and her

hands gripped his muscled back, pulling him on top of her, pillowing his weight against her softness. She wanted to be one with him; she wanted nothing to separate them. Time and place had ceased to exist as they created their own world.

When he broke the kiss Iverson nuzzled his face into her blouse, his lips nipping along the slope of her breasts, and he delighted in the sighs of pleasure that escaped her lips. He enjoyed her sensuous squirming and her quivers of passion. Tenderly his tongue began to trace the outline of her bra, and she gasped, her stomach contracting with knots of desire.

Her hands, working with fevered accuracy and purpose, shoved under his shirt, pushing it up. Then she surprised both of them. She squirmed and moved, toppling him over so that she became the aggressor, treating him to her love strokes.

Then she leaned back on her knees, rocking on her feet. With slow deliberation she unbuttoned her blouse; she flexed it off her shoulders, tossed it aside. She sat there for a moment, casting all fears aside, letting Iverson look at her, burning in the heat of his passionate gaze.

She bent over him. "I want to take your shirt off."

Immediately he sat up, his hands lifting up the bottom of the sweater. Before he could pull it over his head, however, Melissa stopped his movements, smiling, shaking her head, repeating, "*I* want to take it off."

She lifted it over his head, tossing it on the growing heap. Iverson leaned forward, his arms circling her back, his hands touching the clasp of her bra. Again she shook her head, pushing him down with the tips of her fingers.

"Let me." She reached back and unsnapped the offending garment. Crossing her arms in front of herself, she clasped the straps and pulled them down, freeing her breasts from their lacy halter.

She continued to kneel beside him, and she watched him. She saw the passionate glaze that covered his auburn eyes; she felt the heat that permeated from them. She felt his touch. He sat up, propped on one elbow, his other hand adoring the beautiful femininity of her breasts between his thumb and index finger.

Then with only a slight movement his head lifted, and he took one of her nipples in his mouth. With a gentle twist, he held her in his arms, sucking on her breast. With each tug Melissa gasped her pleasure, feeling her desire as it effused throughout her body, beginning at the core of her being. She wrapped her hands around his head, and she ran her fingers through his hair, her body quivering with passion.

But when he nudged her down, she again shook her head. "No," she whispered, "I'm not through yet." She stood to her feet, unsnapping her jeans, then unzipping them. She kicked them off, dropping them at her feet. She pushed her hands beneath the elastic and the filmy nylon of her panties, sliding them over her hips and down her legs.

Iverson's eyes were dark with desire as he looked at her beauty. And although he wanted to make love to her, he also wanted her to make love to him. He didn't infringe on her ministrations of love. He watched as she again knelt beside him, leaning over him. Beginning at his eyes, she softly deposited hot, feverish kisses over his face, his neck, his shoulders, his chest. Down his torso to his stomach . . .

"We need to discard these jeans," she whispered.

Iverson quivered beneath her touch, and his hand, cupping the nape of her neck, spread through her hair, and he pulled her face up to his. "Oh, God, Melissa," he ground out in a thick, husky voice, "remind me never to call you a little girl again. You're a full-grown woman."

She laughed softly, gasping as he pulled her lips over his in a hot, open kiss. "I told you so."

Then neither said a word as they discovered the wonder of their bodies, as they explored and as they aroused. Melissa's hands touched the waistband of Iverson's jeans, and she wrestled with the fastening until she unclasped it. She unzipped them and pulled them open, seeing only the white triangle of his briefs. She gently traced her fingers back and forth over the firm protrusion.

Then Iverson could stand no more of the tormenting teasing. He shifted her aside, and he took off his jeans and underwear, fully revealing himself for her, lying back, letting her adore him with her eyes. Melissa lowered her face, again covering his stomach with kisses, reveling in her prowess to arouse him, delighting in the feel of his hot moist flesh.

"Flesh and blood," she whispered, tentatively touching his pulsating flesh, reverently stroking his thighs. "Yet when I first met you, I thought you were granite through and through."

"Not granite, darling," he denied softly, taking her into his arms, pulling her face to his. "All flesh and blood."

Their lips touched again, and his hands cupped the firmness of her breasts, kneading them, building up the tension of desire in her body as he kindled the same desires in himself. And then he turned, pulling Melissa under him.

Their coming together was wild and beyond anything Melissa had dreamed. Never had a man touched her soul; never had anyone delved beyond the physical to touch the spiritual. As she and Iverson climbed their mountain of love together, she closed her eyes, their bodies tied into one mass of humanity by the circling bands of arms and legs, their lips bound together in hot, wet kisses, their souls bonded together in ecstasy.

Afterward they lay in dreamy lethargy, talking, sharing all the small but intimate details of lovers. Then they jumped to their feet, racing to the waterfall, showering and shivering in the icy mountain stream, making love again, loving each other all over again. Their world was complete, Melissa thought dreamily, glad their consummation had taken place here. Here, where they were cradled by the majestic mountain and caressed by the sun and the wind, their union was sanctioned by the voluminous white clouds that floated lazily in the blue sky and they were protected and sheltered by the verdant canopy of green forest.

Later, hand in hand, they slowly retraced their steps back to the inn. Melissa had climbed her mountain; she had found her man. And perhaps she had found her love.

Softly Iverson whispered in her ear, "Shall we spend the night and go fishing in the morning?"

"Oh, yes," she cried happily, not wanting to break this beautiful oneness they were creating, not wanting to return to their everyday world too soon. She lifted her face and smiled up at him. She wasn't ready to share her discovery with the world yet. Then suddenly she exclaimed, "But I don't have any clothes for tomorrow." She looked down at her shirt and jeans. "Just these."

Iverson laughed her opposition away. "We'll wash them. Mary Jane and Mr. R. L. do have some modern conveniences, two of which include a washer and dryer."

When they arrived back at the inn Mary Jane invited them to eat dinner with her and her husband,

R. L. With no hesitation she and Iverson agreed. As quickly as Melissa had fallen in love with Mary Jane, she fell in love with R. L. He was a soft-spoken man, who was dressed in a long-sleeved flannel shirt, overalls, and a battered hat. Never in a hurry, he ambled slowly from place to place. In his soft country vernacular he entertained them through the meal, and afterward they sat on the front porch, watching night as it gently settled around them.

Listening to the tales R. L. and Mary Jane told, Iverson and Melissa sat in the big swing, gently swaying back and forth. Finally, however, Iverson said, "Well, folks, I reckon it's time that we turned in."

"Since you like to fish," R. L. drawled, looking at Melissa, "I wonder if you'd be interested in going fishing tomorrow?" He reached up, taking his hat off, and scratching his head, grinning. "At my favorite fishing hole?"

"Could we?" Melissa exclaimed, looking up at Iverson. "Please?"

"How can I say no?" He grinned. "It looks like it's two to one, and Mr. R. L. has never offered to take me to his favorite fishing hole."

While the three discussed the coming excursion, Mary Jane quietly slipped into the house, returning with a brown paper bag which she placed in Melissa's hand at an inconspicuous time. "Thought you might need this tonight," she whispered. "It gets mighty cold up here in the mountains."

"What is it?" Melissa asked curiously, keeping her voice low while peeping into the bag.

In the light that filtered from the living room onto the porch, Melissa could see the lid of one of Mary

Jane's eyes come down in a wink. "Just wait and see. It's not the most romantic thing in the world, but it'll sure come in handy when the fire's burned down and Iverson's asleep."

CHAPTER SIX

Melissa, garbed in Mary Jane's flannel nightgown with its high neckline and long sleeves, was drying the breakfast dishes and putting them into the cabinet when she heard the door open. Looking up, she saw Iverson enter the cabin with his arms full of fishing gear. "Every time I see you coming through a door you're loaded down," she teased.

"And it's always your fault," he complained lightly, closing the door with his foot as he moved toward the table. "Night before last I had to tuck you in bed; yesterday morning I had to feed you, and this morning I was out washing your clothes so you would have something to wear." He held her jeans and blouse in one hand, her underwear and socks in the other. "And I do mean, woman, all your clothes."

"Is this the first time that you've stooped to perform menial tasks?"

"Nope. But it's the first time that I've washed a woman's intimate apparel."

Moving closer to him, she reached for her clothes, but he tossed them on the bed, lifting a hand to catch the nosepiece of her glasses and pull them off her face. As he set them on the table, his other arm circled her shoulders, and he drew her into his arms. His auburn eyes glittered with amusement. "And I got some strange looks from the Barkers."

111

Melissa chuckled. "You should have let me do that. I hadn't thought about their reaction."

"Not only was it a first for them to see me washing," Iverson declared, "but to see me washing a lady's unmentionables." Melissa's chuckle turned into rich laughter, and she laid her face on his chest. "I think," he said, his hands sliding down, cupping the roundness of her buttocks, "my image has been shattered. R. L. will never see me in the same light again."

"Nor will I," Melissa added, burrowing herself closer to him, wondering how much longer she would see this side of him. "Totally emasculated." She giggled, lifting a hand to his chest to trace a thread of color in his shirt with the tip of her finger.

"Totally."

"Does it bother you?"

"No. My only concern at the moment is your image of me. What do you think about me?"

"I think you can pop corn wonderfully," she retorted, trying to keep her voice light even as elation raced through her body. "And I love the way you so deftly snap the cap off a beer bottle. And—"

"No, Melissa, no jokes. No teasing. I want to know. What has this weekend meant to you? Do we have a future together?" All masks were gone, and Melissa could see a touch of vulnerability in his expression; she could hear the hint of uncertainty in his voice.

"You're asking me?" she countered softly, almost choking on her words as emotion overwhelmed her. "I —I thought—" She stopped, then began again. "You surprise me, Iverson. You're so different from what I had imagined. So different from my first impression."

"In what way?"

"I wouldn't have thought you would be concerned with my feelings," she said. "I—I thought you rode roughshod over people, disregarding their wishes and

112

desires. I thought you were the type to take what you wanted regardless of the consequences."

"According to many people, I am all that and more." Clasping her hand in his, he tugged gently, leading her to the chair in front of the fireplace. He sat down and he pulled her into his lap. "I'm no different from anyone else. I ride roughshod when I have to, and there are times when my interests dictate my disregarding others' wishes and desires. And I learned a long time ago, Melissa, that I had to fight for myself. I quickly learned that a person who tries to please everyone ends up pleasing no one, himself included." He stared into the dwindling flames of the fire. "And I do know what I want, Melissa. I want to have an affair with you. But that's my question. I want to know what you want; I want to know how you feel about us."

"Not about you?" she inquired curiously.

"No, it's a little too soon for you to really know and understand me. Right now we're sailing high on the newness of our loving. I'll leave that question until a little later when we know each other better. When we've got both feet on the ground and have seen each other at our best and at our worst."

"What are you asking me then?"

"Do you want to be around me long enough to see the worst, to see if you can love the worst as easily as you can love the best?"

"I think, Iverson Gerrick, that I have seen you at your very worst. Nothing could be worse than your barking and carrying on about the employees from Day's Work."

"That wasn't my worst," he snapped. "That was the worst of that little agency you work for. Those women were atrocious, and I would do the same thing again if it were necessary." Melissa cringed as she heard the harsh criticism. What would he think if he knew the truth about her affiliation with Day's Work?

"Now, back to the question at hand," he said. "Do you want us to go on from here?"

Yes, Melissa thought, gazing into his face, she did want to go on from here. But she wondered about the wisdom of her doing so. It was hard for her to reconcile the two facets of Iverson's personality that she had seen. It was difficult for her to accept the overbearing and autocratic executive dictatorship he wielded. But it was so easy for her to love the man—the gentle, lovable mountain man.

"Well?" he prompted, watching the telltale expressions as they flitted across her face. "Do we go on from here?"

"Yes."

"Good." His face lowered, his lips going straight to hers. After several lingering kisses he began to plant quick kisses on her lips and on her face; then he stood, setting her on her feet. "Get your clothes on, woman, if you want to go fishing. I promise you a day that you'll never forget."

"What if I don't put my clothes on?" she teased.

Iverson chuckled deeply and richly. "So much the better, and my promise still holds." He leaned over, kissing the tip of her nose. "R. L. will be highly insulted and disappointed though."

"And we can't disappoint R. L., can we?" Melissa asked, her arms closing around his waist.

"For this we can," Iverson sighed, his hands beginning to roam her body, quickly igniting the fires of desire. Then his lips lowered again, tenderly molding themselves to the softness of hers, and as Melissa pressed herself against him, she lost herself in their kiss.

114

Finally Iverson mumbled, "What's it to be, my darling?"

"Must I choose?" Melissa whispered. "Can't we have both?"

"You may have both, my darling." Laughing, Iverson stood to his feet, swinging Melissa up in his arms and carrying her across the room. Gently he lowered her onto the bed, leaning over, looking at her for a long time before he straightened up to undress. Mesmerized, Melissa watched the pieces of clothing as he peeled them from his body; then she looked at his splendid nakedness, a splendor that was enhanced because she saw him through the eyes of love.

He slid on the bed beside her, his hands running up her legs beneath the yards of soft flannel, pulling Mary Jane's nightgown over her head before his lips sought hers in a deep kiss. The playing was over, the teasing and the tormenting done away with. Putting everything out of their minds, they made love with their mouths, their hands, their entire bodies.

In between the warm, moist, open-mouthed kisses, Iverson tenderly nipped his lips over hers, and he breathed love words. All the time his fingers ran up her thighs across her hips; then his palm flattened on her belly, and she writhed in ecstatic agony, soft moans slipping through her lips. She arched as she felt him move, as she felt his lips feathering across her breasts, across her midriff, down her stomach, up again.

Her eyes closed, she lay on her back, her head on the thick pillows, turning from side to side. Iverson half-sitting on the side of the bed, half-lying across her, brushed love on her breasts, his lips and his tongue tenderly nipping and sucking.

When Iverson lifted his head, she opened her eyes and stared at him, her eyes glazed with passion. His eyes also glowed and Melissa could see the same wanting in him that flowed through her. Her hands cupped his face, and her fingers tenderly stroked his freshly shaven cheeks.

Withdrawing from her grasp, he lowered his face again, his lips burning a trail of desire across her midriff, back and forth, the path getting wider and wider, igniting every nerve ending, sparking a fire in the very depths of her soul. She ached for his touch, for the fullness only his possession could bring to her. And her wanting began in the nucleus of her being, bridging her sexual and her spiritual desires.

At the same time that his lips burned their brand across her midriff, his hand began a slow erotic journey from her knee to her inner thigh. She writhed; she groaned; her hands tangled in his hair. And he listened to her pleas; he followed her directives until she was begging him for completion.

She moved, lifting her shoulders, wrapping her hands around his shoulders, pulling his face to hers, fevered lips seeking fevered lips. Smoothly he turned until he was lying beside her, and while they kissed her hands slid down his chest and across his tight stomach.

As their lips moved against each other's in the dance of love, as their breathing became deeper and more ragged, as their kisses became wetter and hotter, she whetted his desires to her fevered pitch, blatantly stroking him, making him beg for completion also. He wrenched his mouth from hers, and his fingers ran gently through her hair. He moved his body, and they came together.

As they loved, they made love. Again they scaled their mountain, that beautiful mountain of love that only they could create. They climbed with no hesitation in their steps. They were confident in their strength and dauntless in their direction. Although equally matched, Iverson made sure that Melissa reached the peak, made sure her needs were fulfilled, made sure she gasped her pleasure; then he took his and collapsed on her.

So precious was the moment to Melissa that she cradled Iverson's body against hers, loving him, thanking him, whispering words of love to him. Then he braced his hands on either side of her head, lifted himself up, and looked into her face. "Thank you, my darling." He lowered his lips to hers in an infinitely sweet kiss. With tender love strokes and words, he slowly led her from the lofty peak, and finally they lay still, side by side, bathed in purest love.

Later they showered together and then dressed and walked to the inn to get the goodies that Mary Jane had packed for them. Laughing and talking, they quickly loaded the car.

"This about it?" Iverson asked, putting the ice chest into the trunk.

Pushing around him, Melissa made a quick inventory, enumerating the items. Suddenly she squealed, "No, that's not all."

"What did I forget?"

"My cane pole," she called over her shoulder, racing toward the cabin.

Iverson grimaced cheerfully, teasing her. "Why do you want to fish with that when R. L. has loaned us his very best."

"Because Miss Mary Jane gave me this pole, and it's her very best. I'll bet you that I'll catch more with the pole than you'll catch with the rod and reel, and I'll bet even if you do catch more, mine will be the bigger."

Iverson's laughter echoed behind her, causing happiness to radiate her countenance. She skipped up the steps and darted across the room to the patio doors, where she had left the pole. Grabbing it, she hastily rewrapped the string as she spun around to retrace her steps. At that moment the telephone rang, causing her to stop. She looked at the offending black instrument, and she debated.

After it had rung the third time, she decided to answer it. She picked up the receiver, but before she could open her mouth to speak, she heard R. L.'s slow drawl. "Reckon he's not in his room, Mr. Bradley. Can I take a message?"

"Yes, Nicole is trying to reach him. She says it's very important. I wouldn't tell her where Iverson was, but I took her number and promised that I would give her message to him."

While Bradley recited the phone number, Melissa laid the receiver back in the cradle. Why was Nicole calling Iverson again? Melissa wondered. Angry and upset, she walked to the car, wondering just how much of a relationship Nicole would allow her and Iverson to build. When Melissa reached the car, she handed the pole to Iverson, and watched as he tucked it in the backseat, letting it jut out the front window.

"Here you are," Mary Jane announced, walking down the steps of the house, holding a jug in the air. "Best apple cider in the country, Melissa. Chill it and feast on its sharpness. Fixed it myself."

Graciously Melissa took the proffered jug and walked to the back of the car, opening the chest to rearrange their drinks. Just as she snapped the lid to, R. L. slowly ambled to the edge of the veranda. He lifted his gnarled hand, wiping the snuff stains from the corners of his mouth, and he spit over the edge before he spoke in that soft drawl.

"Your pa called, Iverson. Left a message."

"Okay," Iverson returned, slamming the trunk

118

shut. Briskly he sprinted onto the porch to stand closer to R. L., his back to Melissa.

Melissa stood as still as a statue, listening as R. L. mumbled to Iverson. Because Iverson blocked the older man from her view and because R. L. had lowered his voice, she couldn't understand what he was saying, but she knew. She waited for Iverson's reply, Nicole's voice again sounding in her mind, the words haunting her with their emphatic refrain. *He'll return my call as soon as he gets the message.* Surely Iverson wouldn't return Nicole's call, she thought. Surely not today. Not after what they had shared together.

Iverson turned and gazed at Melissa, his eyes dark and brooding. "I've got to make a call," he said, never breaking visual contact with her. "Business."

Not wanting to believe what she heard, Melissa gasped, but she wasn't aware that she had emitted the sound until she felt Mary Jane's arm slide around her shoulder.

"Nothing's ever the way it looks," Mary Jane explained. "Don't get in a dither till you know all the facts."

"Thanks," Melissa whispered, pulling away slowly. "Tell Iverson that I'll be waiting in our cabin for him."

She wasn't sure how long she stood in the kitchen waiting. An eternity would seem short in comparison. Finally, however, Iverson walked into the room, his face somber and withdrawn. Suddenly the day didn't seem as sunny and warm as it had earlier. Nor was the room as bright and cheerful.

He walked to where she stood, placing his hands on her shoulders, looking into her face a long time before he spoke. "I'm—I'm sorry, Melissa, but I—we've got to go."

Melissa nodded. "Somehow or other, Iverson, I knew you were going to say that." She smiled, holding

119

her shoulders erect, stiffening her spine. She tensed, but she didn't immediately flinch away from his touch. "The project?"

He nodded.

Melissa could have forgiven him anything but lying. She quickly twisted out of his arms and ducked around him, heading for the door. "I guess we'd better start unpacking the car then."

"Melissa"—his arms shot out and grabbed her, his hands settling like vises on her shoulders, pulling her back to him—"I'm sorry. I didn't want our weekend to end like this."

She shrugged, trying to climb through the mounds of disappointment that had piled on her. "Can't be helped. Like you said, business."

"Something's wrong with you," he mused, his eyes raking over her face, looking for a clue to her inner feelings.

"Of course something's wrong with me. I'm disappointed. I had planned on our having the day together."

"No," he asserted, "it's more than that. You have a right to regret our having to leave. But you're more than upset, more than disappointed. You act as if you're angry. Don't be. There'll be other weekends."

"Yeah," she agreed dispiritedly, "other weekends that will be interrupted by calls like this." What she really wanted to say was, No, Iverson, there will be no other weekends that will be interrupted with calls from Nicole. Instead, she jerked away from him.

"I do have to earn a living," he said impatiently, not understanding her anger, irritated at what he considered to be childish behavior. "And I do want Whitman's cooperation."

"Whitman!" Melissa exclaimed. "What's Whitman got to do with this?"

Iverson didn't answer immediately; rather, he lifted a hand, rubbing the nape of his neck, slowly walking across the carpet to the open patio doors, standing with his back to Melissa. He wanted to tell her the truth, but he was afraid to tell her that his call had been to Nicole. She didn't understand the type of person Nicole was, and she wouldn't understand Nicole's machinations.

"I've got to see Whitman immediately."

"Whitman," Melissa whispered. "You're leaving here to go meet with Whitman?"

Iverson nodded. "I would put it off until tomorrow, Melissa, but I can't." He didn't intend to let Nicole mess up the negotiations he was working on.

"Do you think I'm a fool?" Melissa blazed, her anger out of control. "I know better than that. How dare you lie to me! I know Nicole called you. She's the one you're going to meet."

Iverson was incredulous, and his eyes widened and darkened. "You listened in on my call!"

"No, I did not. I was in here when the phone rang, and I picked it up to answer it. That's when I heard your father talking to R. L."

"You don't understand."

"No," Melissa said, "I don't. But I want you to understand this. I'm not going to compete with Nicole for your attention." She shook her head wearily. "I'm vulnerable where you're concerned, Iverson. My body's already totally involved with you, and my heart's on its way there. I'm not going to let you hurt me this way."

"Melissa, please listen."

She walked to the door, closing her hand over the doorknob. "What haven't you told me, Iverson?" she asked quietly, not waiting for an answer. "Instead of business with Whitman, it's pleasure with Nicole."

Before she knew what had happened, he had come over to her and had braced her against the wall with his body.

"We're not leaving like this. You're going to listen to me."

"Am I given no choice?" she gritted between clenched teeth as his hands again clamped over her shoulders and pinched into her flesh.

"No," he distinctly enunciated, clipping his words. "What we shared yesterday and last night and this morning takes the choice out of your hands."

"My choice is restricted only because you're holding me by brute force and won't let me go." She flexed her shoulders, and his hands fell limply to his sides. "I don't know what kind of arrangement you and Nicole have, and I wish I didn't care. But, no matter, you can leave me out."

"Although Nicole is the one who placed the call," Iverson insisted, "it was regarding business. It concerns Whitman and me. Believe it or not, she does pose a threat to the project."

"Does she?" Melissa asked skeptically.

Iverson didn't attempt to argue with her. "Why can't you trust me?"

"Because you haven't earned it. All you've got so far is my contempt. Nicole called you before we left the Homestead. Then she had you paged by your father, and you couldn't get to that telephone fast enough to return her call." She laughed bitterly. "As I see it, you and Nicole are two of a kind. Both of you seem to delight in playing these little games, seeing who can outmaneuver the other. Well, Iverson Gerrick, mark this down in your little black book—I won't be a pawn used by either one of you."

"You're faulting me," he blazed, anger in his voice, "for not telling you the whole truth and for protecting

122

my business interests, yet you seem to make a habit of listening in on my telephone calls."

"Quite by accident and quite informative both times," she returned, not the least intimidated by his fury, motivated by her own. "She really keeps tabs on you, doesn't she?"

"I've explained it to you," he thundered, "and I've told you the truth. I've done all that I can do." His voice was every bit as cold and hard as hers.

She moved around the cabin. "You're too smart to make an open play for Nicole, but you know that her interest will start flaming if you have a new woman in your life." She tossed her head, her hair swirling around her face. "Is that why you told her we were lovers? Whetting her interest, Iverson?"

"How can you think something like this?"

"You said she wants only the forbidden or the unobtainable. It sure looks like you're making yourself unobtainable, doesn't it, Iverson? Instead of taking me fishing, you were fishing with me, luring Nicole into your camp."

"God!" Iverson grated, finally goaded into retaliation. "You do think I'm contemptible!" He shook his head in perplexity. "Can't you understand what I'm trying to tell you? Nicole is sick. She's out to ruin me if she can, Melissa: I've got to protect myself and the project."

"That's right," she spat out contemptuously, "protect that project at all costs."

"I need Whitman," Iverson explained, "and Nicole is going to see to it that I don't get him unless I get her also. She's doing all this on the pretense of caring about him and his company. In reality, she wants a piece of the pie. She couldn't care less about Tom or his company, Whitman Transportation International. They had an affair when he was married, but once he divorced his wife, Nicole was through with him. His availability diminished his desirability. But she's still involved with him—now that she knows I'm interested in doing business with him. She wants to be a partner in the venture—or she plans to ruin any chance of it coming to be. There's nothing Nicole would love more than seeing me come to heel. All she's ever cared about was business."

"Evidently she's blind," Melissa belted unmercifully. "You're already there. And if you're not, all she has to do is call and you come running." Melissa remembered that a month ago she had planned to bring him to heel also.

"I've got to get to Whitman before Nicole does, Melissa. I don't trust her, and I know she's got something up her sleeve. Please try to understand."

"I do," she whispered softly. "I really do."

"Are you seeing what you think is the worst side of me?" he asked.

She smiled sadly, regretfully, neither agreeing nor disagreeing with him. She walked into the kitchen, filling the coffeemaker with water and grounds. Then she turned it on.

Iverson followed her, opening the cabinet, taking down two cups. "I think you're being unfair, Melissa. Because you're disappointed and hurt, you're seeing things only from your point of view. You're not giving me a fair deal."

"Granted," she replied. She heard Iverson as he set the cups on the table, and she heard the chair as it scraped against the floor, but she didn't look at him. "I want equal time, Iverson. I don't want to play second to a job or a proposal or an ex-wife."

"I hear what you're saying, but you're not hearing what I'm saying, Melissa. I'm doing what I've got to do to protect my interests—both you and the business."

She finally turned to look at him. "You're meeting with Nicole, aren't you? And you're afraid to tell me because you don't want to upset the apple cart."

"No, I'm meeting with Whitman to go over the proposal again—"

She finished his statement. "But Nicole will be there."

He nodded. "Probably."

In a silence that grew heavier by the passing seconds, she lifted the pot and walked to the table, filling their cups. Then she sat across the table from him. Neither spoke as they drank their coffee, and neither looked at the other. Both stared down at the table.

Finally Iverson raised his head, asking, "Would you go with me?"

"Last-ditch effort to appease me so negotiations will go without a hitch?" she said dully.

"No." He sighed. "I hadn't asked you before because I wanted to shield you from Nicole. She could cause a scene and I didn't want her to hurt you."

Melissa lifted her face, adjusting her glasses on the bridge of her nose at the same time she spoke. "You think I can't take care of myself?"

"You've never been up against someone like Nicole," he parried evasively.

"You don't have much confidence or faith in me."

"I was only trying to protect you."

"Perhaps you were," she acquiesced.

"You'll go?"

She shook her head. "It will probably be better if I didn't."

"You're not going to allow Nicole to come between us, are you?" he asked.

"No, I'm not, but I'm wondering if you will."

125

CHAPTER SEVEN

Melissa entered the Gerrick Building early Monday morning, walking directly to her office, not even stopping by the lounge for her usual cup of coffee. She dropped her briefcase and purse on the desk, and she moved to the window, staring at Asheville. Although she had spent a restless night, she successfully camouflaged the telltale signs of sleeplessness with makeup, and she had wisely chosen a beautiful spring skirt and sweater in pastel greens and yellows to accent her golden eyes and sun-streaked hair.

The weekend that had begun so promisingly had ended so quickly. And nothing had been resolved between her and Iverson by the time he dropped her off at the house yesterday.

He had walked her to the door, setting her suitcase down as he turned the key in the lock. "I'd like to come in, but I don't have time," he explained in a flat tone, having exhausted all his arguments and persuasions. "Sure you won't come with me?" When she had shaken her head, he said, "I'll call you later."

"I may not be home," she told him. "I'll probably take Penny and Charles up on their previous invitation." She smiled lamely, explaining, "My mother's there. Dinner with the family and an evening of games with Lane and Randal."

Iverson had nodded. "That'll be better than sitting

126

around the house by yourself." He lifted his hands and gently cupped her face. "I'll see you in the morning."

Although spoken as a statement, Melissa could hear the uncertainty that threaded through his words, and she promised, "In the morning."

Leaning down, he placed his lips on her forehead in a tender gesture of love, and he started to speak. "Melissa, I—"

She didn't let him complete his sentence. She moved her head and lifted her hand, laying her fingers over his mouth. Smiling tenderly, she looked into his face. "I think I understand, Iverson, but it still hurts. It's a little too soon. Give me some time."

He had nodded. "See you in the morning, darling."

"Good morning, Melissa." Miss Bromley's crisp words jarred Melissa back to the present. "Since you didn't stop by the lounge for your coffee, I thought you might like this." She set a paper cup on Melissa's desk and sat down in the nearest chair.

Turning from the window and moving toward her desk, Melissa said, "Thanks. Just what I need before I jump into those papers Iverson wants for Whitman."

"Speaking of Iverson," Orlaine said, taking a swallow of coffee. "He called me last night and left a message for you. He wanted to talk with you himself, but he had forgotten to get your brother-in-law's last name and didn't know how to reach you."

Melissa laughed. "And I didn't think of giving it to him."

Orlaine nodded, not quite sure what had passed between Iverson and Melissa, but whatever it was, it had affected both of them. For the first time since Melissa had come to work for the Gerrick Corporation, she was quiet and withdrawn, not herself at all. And last night when Iverson called, Orlaine had been surprised at his concern, and she was certain it was personal interest for Melissa that had spurred the call.

"Iverson wanted me to be the one to tell you that he had to fly to Miami."

Melissa held the rim of the cup up to her lips, saying, "The project."

Orlaine nodded. "It was urgent. Both he and Bradley flew out with Dillson yesterday." She smiled, pulling a sheet of paper out of her pocket. "Iverson wants you to get all this together for him as soon as possible. Said he'd call you at about ten to let you know if you're to join him."

As soon as Orlaine left, Melissa went to work getting all the material Iverson had requisitioned. Glad that he had thought of sending a message through Orlaine, Melissa eagerly awaited his call, hoping that he would want her to join him. When the call came, however, it was from Bradley rather than Iverson.

"Iverson's tied up right now," Bradley explained, "and can't get away. He's going to send a courier for the information, so have it packaged and ready to go. Also," he added before he hung up, "Iverson said to tell you he'll call as soon as he can."

Smiling as she replaced the receiver, Melissa hastily shuffled all the material into a manila file folder and labeled it. Then she dropped it into a large mailing envelope, addressed it, and laid it on the corner of her desk, waiting for the courier service.

"Ready for a break?" Orlaine called, swinging her head around the door.

"Go on," Melissa said, "I'll be right down. I just want to make sure that I've got everything done. Won't take me a sec."

Hardly had Orlaine disappeared down the hall, than Melissa heard a soft feminine voice, a voice she recognized instantly. "Good morning, Miss Phillips."

Lifting her head, Melissa stared at the woman who lounged elegantly in the opened door. She knew it was Nicole Lambert. "Good morning," Melissa greeted her, surprised that her voice sounded normal. Nothing could have prepared her for the beauty of the woman. Her blond hair was parted on the side and hung in shining, silken sheets on both sides of the slender face. Her lips, curved in a smile that never reached her eyes, were a bright, vivid red, and her blue eyes glowed.

Clutching a small black purse in her left hand, she took a step forward, her tall, slender figure gracefully bringing her closer to Melissa's desk. The sky-blue sweater dress, the same color as her eyes, fit her body snugly, and it bespoke extravagance. The tiny gold chain that draped around her hips matched the chains that hung around her neck.

"I believe you have a package for me," she said in that sultry voice that had haunted Melissa ever since last Friday evening.

Melissa smiled, leaning back in her chair, overtly studying Nicole. "Do I?"

The expression on Nicole's face didn't change, but the voice became acid and hard. "Don't play games with me, Ms. Phillips. I don't have time for your nonsense."

Melissa took her glasses off, leaned across her desk, and pulled a tissue from a wooden dispenser. Holding both earpieces in her left hand, she began to clean the lenses. Never looking up, she said, "You've misjudged me, Nicole. I don't play games. I play for keeps."

"Are you telling me something?" Nicole asked, stopping at the edge of the desk.

Melissa held her glasses up in the air, and she looked through them. "I understand that you're a very astute woman, Nicole. Surely you knew the answer to your question before you asked."

"You're not quite what I had pictured, Melissa"—Nicole chuckled softly, hiding her irritation—"you remind me of a child."

"Do I?" Melissa parried. "Maybe it's because you look so old for your age and I look so young for mine." She slipped her glasses back on, and she looked at the tall, willowy woman who had been Iverson's wife. She laughed. "I'm sure that Iverson would quickly let you know, though, that I'm a woman"—she paused—"in every sense of the word."

"Don't get your hopes up too high where Iverson is concerned," Nicole lashed out venomously, giving vent to her anger. "He's never been seriously interested in any woman but me."

"Until now," Melissa returned, unwilling to let Nicole push her around. She had never been one to retreat, and she wasn't going to start now.

"Do you really think you can interest Iverson?" Nicole spat out, raking her eyes contemptuously over Melissa's slight frame. "Look at the difference between you and me! Do you think after having had a woman like me Iverson would be satisfied with you?"

Melissa replied so quietly, Nicole had to strain to hear. "I've been thinking about that ever since you walked through the door, Nicole."

"You're nothing like me. You couldn't hope to compete with me," Nicole taunted.

"No, I'm not, thank God!" Melissa exclaimed. "And that should tell you something, Nicole. Iverson's not pining over you, if that's what you're hoping, and he's finally getting you out of his system. He's not looking for a substitute. He's looking for a wife and a lover. His choosing me proves that he wanted someone different from you."

Melissa wasn't all that sure what Iverson was looking for, and she wasn't sure that she was his choice, but she refused to let Nicole treat her so shabbily. No matter how frightened she was, no matter how unsure, she refused to cower in front of Nicole Lambert. If she went down, she would go down fighting.

"You're in love with him!" Nicole exclaimed, her face twisting in a grimace. Melissa just shrugged; she didn't acknowledge or refute the statement. Nicole began to laugh, and this time Melissa could tell that she had shattered the other woman's aplomb. The sound was high and shrill. "But you'll never get Iverson. I'll see to that. All I have to do is snap my fingers, and I'll have him back."

"Perhaps that was true until this weekend," Melissa replied with more bravery than she really felt, but once she'd taken the bull by the horns she refused to turn him loose. "Now things will be different."

Nicole laid her palms on Melissa's desk and leaned closer to her. "I thought you were an intelligent woman, Melissa. If Iverson's calling me Friday night wasn't enough proof of my control over him, surely yesterday's call was. Did you realize that he left you and immediately came over to my house?"

Melissa's heart sank to her feet as she thought about the truth in Nicole's taunt, but she stood her ground. "If he did, it's because Tom was there."

Nicole's laughter mocked her. "Wouldn't you like to think so? But tonight, Melissa, I'll be with him in Miami, and Tom won't be with us. Come tomorrow, we'll see exactly where you stand with Iverson Gerrick." She straightened up and lifted her hand, flipping her hair out of her eyes, which were bright and glittered with hatred. "Now, if you'll just give me the file."

Melissa shook her head. "I can't, Nicole. Iverson is sending a courier for it."

"Since I'm flying to Miami, I'll take it myself.

131

There's no need to wait for a courier. After all, I'm party to the negotiations now."

"I can't," Melissa retaliated, wondering if Nicole had finally gotten herself included. "Although the material has been assimilated for Mr. Whitman, Iverson wants it first. I've been instructed to wait for the courier."

Nicole's laughter was bitter. "You can't keep me from reading it. I'll be the first one to see that file no matter who receives it, Iverson or Tom."

Melissa nodded. "Perhaps, but you won't see it before Iverson gets his hands on it unless he calls himself and tells me to release it to you."

"Don't think you'll get away with this," Nicole hissed. "You won't. I'll have your job for this."

Three short light taps at the door stopped Nicole's threat, and both women turned to look at the uniformed young man. "Carl Blanchard with Mercury Express, ma'am. Believe you've got a parcel for us to pick up."

Melissa nodded and smiled at him, holding the envelope in the air. The messenger walked across the room, took the package, and clamped it under his arm as he filled out a receipt. Handing Melissa the clipboard, he said, "Sign right here, please." After she wrote her name across the sheet of paper, Carl tore her copy off and handed it to her. "Thanks, Ms. Phillips. Have a good day." Turning, he walked out of the room.

"You think you've won, don't you, Melissa?" Nicole asked, picking up the conversation where it had been severed.

Melissa shook her head. "I'm not sure that I've won, Nicole, but I think I've chalked up several points."

Nicole spun around, then walked to the door, posing elegantly. "Beware, Melissa. I'm not through with you yet."

Through the rest of the week, Nicole's words haunted Melissa. She knew how important this business project was to Iverson and wondered how far he was willing to go to protect it from Nicole. She wondered how far Nicole was willing to go to destroy it for Iverson if she couldn't get involved in it. On Tuesday, when he called, letting her know the file had arrived, Melissa told him about Nicole's visit.

Iverson commended Melissa's handling of the situation, but he quickly changed the subject, as if he wanted to avoid the subject of Nicole. However, he did tell Melissa that he wouldn't be returning home until the weekend. He and Dillson were flying to the West Coast, and he would also be helping his father transact some business. He told her that he would call her when he arrived home.

Because Melissa was so busy, the week passed quickly. And because she had worked so late every evening, Orlaine had insisted that she take Friday afternoon off. Before she left the office, however, the phone rang.

"Long distance call from Miami on line one, Ms. Phillips. Want to take it?"

"Yes, I'll take it," Melissa replied eagerly. Then she said, "Melissa Phillips."

"Hello, Melissa."

Dear God, Melissa thought, it can't be!

"This is Nicole. I'm calling from the airport in Miami. I just wanted to let you know that Iverson returned here from San Francisco, so we could fly home together." She laughed. "I thought you would want to know. And if I have my way about it, we'll be home tonight and we'll be going to the theater." With-

133

out saying good-bye, Nicole hung up in her ear, her soft laughter mocking Melissa.

Afterward Melissa hadn't even gone home; she drove over to Penny's to spend the evening with her and the children, helping them get packed for a weekend trip. Linda was staying with them overnight so she could leave with them first thing in the morning. Although the boys begged her to spend the night also so she could see them off in the morning, Melissa declined, going home instead.

Exhausted when she arrived at the house, she walked straight to her bedroom, undressed, and went to bed. But it seemed that she had no sooner gone to sleep than the incessant ringing of the doorbell awakened her. She fumbled in the dark for the lamp switch, swinging her feet over the edge of the bed. Yawning and rubbing her hand over her eyes, she reached for her glasses, pushing them on her face as she stumbled across the room, sliding her feet into her slippers. Who could it be? she wondered, picking up her robe, her eyes darting to the clock on the nightstand. It was one o'clock. Surely Linda's weekend trip hadn't ended before it began.

"Coming," she mumbled, pulling her robe around her as she walked, running her hand through her sleep-tousled hair. In no hurry she walked through the hall to the entryway, turning on the porch light. She flipped the night lock, dropped the chain, and twisted the knob, opening the door.

"Ye—" The greeting dribbled into silence, her countenance instantly saturated with her surprise. "Iverson," she whispered, her eyes raking over the man who indolently leaned against the doorframe.

"Where have you been?" he asked, a slight irritation evident in his voice. "I've been trying to call you all evening."

"Out," she evaded, her eyes sweeping over his tuxedo. His tie flapped loosely around his neck, and his jacket hung over his left shoulder, hitched on the index finger of his hand. "Where have you been?" she asked, Nicole's words ringing in her ears.

"To the theater."

"What are you doing here at this time of the morning?" Evidently Nicole had gotten her way.

He shrugged and smiled, his jaws darkened with stubble. "I couldn't sleep, and I wanted to see you." His smile deepened. "Remember, last Friday night you helped me through insomnia."

"I don't happen to have any sleeping pills on hand," she quipped dryly. "I have no problem sleeping myself."

"Miss me?" His voice, low and seductive, blatantly tormented her raw nerves, setting them to tingle throughout her body.

"It was rather quiet around the office this week," she answered. "But we managed to get along very well without you."

"Did you miss me?" he persisted, doggedly hounding her, forcing the issue. He wasn't interested in how well she could manage his office; he had confidence in her ability to handle her job. He was concerned about her feelings for him.

"Yes," she whispered, "I missed you."

"I missed you too. May I come in and talk with you for a while?"

"No," she said, wondering about all Nicole had told her, not wanting to believe it but troubled by it nonetheless. "I don't think it would be a good idea. As you can see, I'm already dressed for bed."

"With the proper encouragement I could be dressed for bed too." Although he teased her, his eyes begged for her understanding. "With just the right word both of us could be undressed and ready for bed."

"Not tonight."

"What if I can't sleep by myself? What if I'm still afraid of the dark?"

Melissa chuckled, her eyes again sweeping over his rumpled tuxedo. "Have you even been home to see if you could sleep?"

He grinned. "I went home."

"What did you do? Go to bed in your clothes."

"I didn't stay. I turned right around and drove over here. I wanted to see you. You're a very restful person to be around, Melissa. And"—he drew a long and deep breath, his weariness coming out in a heavy sigh—"you are very therapeutic. In more than one way." He lifted a hand and gently slid the knuckles down her cheek. "May I come in for a little while and talk?" The movement of his hand stilled, but the erratic beating of Melissa's heart continued in wild abandon, and her blood coursed through her veins. "I'm not asking to go to bed with you, although I would like to." His voice was low and sweet, causing desire to ripple through Melissa, causing her legs suddenly to have the consistency of jelly. "I just need you, Melissa. I'm lonely."

Melissa returned the gaze, her heart and her soul melting to the man's needs, to his request. She nodded, never speaking a word. Then she turned, leaving the door open, walking into the den to switch on the light. Iverson knew this was the closest to an invitation that she would issue; therefore, closing the door behind himself, he followed her down the hall into the large room. Once here, he stood in the middle of the floor, looking at and liking the homey clutter.

"I'd forgotten about your mother," he said quietly,

dropping his coat on the sofa. "I didn't awaken her, did I?"

Melissa shook her head. "No, she spends most of her weekends with my stepsister, Penny, and her family. As soon as she left work today she headed over there. They're getting up early in the morning and are going to Carowinds."

"You don't mind being left behind?" he asked, walking around the room, studying the paintings and wall decorations before he moved to one of the large chairs in front of the television.

"No," Melissa lied, "I had other plans for my evening." Again her eyes swept over his evening attire, and Nicole's words returned to haunt her.

"Such as?" Iverson questioned, sitting down on a rocker, pushing back, closing his eyes.

"What if I were to inquire into your evening?" she countered.

"I'd answer," he returned, opening his eyes, looking across the softly lit room at her, grinning. "I'd enjoy it if you'd get personal with me. Now, answer *my* question." His injunction was like satin smoothly polishing away the dusty residue of Melissa's anger and her uncertainty.

Again it felt as if her heart turned somersaults in her chest, and her breathing was restricted and painful. "I was at Penny's."

"Did you enjoy the evening?" The soft question was whispered across the room.

"Yes." She lowered her face, drawing imaginary designs on the counter with her fingertips. "Did you enjoy the theater?" The question asked, she waited with bated breath for his answer. She had thought about him all evening, wondering if he was with Nicole.

"No," he returned, "unlike you, I didn't enjoy my evening. I couldn't concentrate on the play. I kept

137

thinking about a certain young lady with whom I would have rather been, but whom I couldn't find. I couldn't get her off my mind."

"Why didn't you call her and ask her to go with you?"

"I did. The minute I arrived in town I began calling, but I never got an answer. Not wanting to spend a lonely evening feeling sorry for myself, I accepted a friend's invitation and went to the theater."

Nicole! Melissa thought.

"But I couldn't concentrate on the play," he continued. "I kept thinking about her pixie face and her upturned nose sprinkled with freckles. I kept seeing those large honey-brown eyes with flickers of devilment in them." So gentle and so sweet were his visual strokes, that even though she didn't want to, Melissa could feel his hands on her face.

"I kept thinking about her smile; it radiates from her very heart and soul. I kept hearing her soft peals of laughter." He had laid bare his soul, and stood emotionally undressed. He wondered how she would respond. "I kept calling her house all through the evening, but I never received an answer."

"What about the young lady whom you were with? Surely she was woman enough to keep your mind occupied?" Melissa said.

"Yes," Iverson replied, genuinely amused, "she was certainly woman enough to keep my mind occupied."

"She didn't mind your making the phone calls?"

He chuckled. "I didn't ask her permission. To be totally honest, I'm not romantically interested in her, nor she with me. Both of us were lonely and wanted a shoulder to cry on."

"What did you need to cry about?" Melissa asked, her heart suddenly much lighter as Nicole's threats and taunts faded away.

"The woman I'm interested in is terribly love-shy, and she misunderstands me. I'm afraid she's misjudged me."

"Has she?" Melissa whispered hoarsely.

"Dunno," he mumbled. "I thought maybe I'd find out tonight." His voice lowered an octave, and the thick, raspy tones flowed over Melissa, touching her, setting her on fire. "Although I was with a woman tonight, Melissa, and surrounded by all those people, I was alone. I needed you because you're the only one who can take away my loneliness. I feel the whole world is where you are."

"Iverson," Melissa begged, "please don't."

"Don't what, Melissa?" he asked, agilely sprinting out of the chair, crossing the room in long strides, and pulling her into his arms. "Don't tell you how I feel about you? Try to pretend that we can be just friends? Try to push aside all we've shared together? Try to muddle through this weekend as best I can without your company? Perhaps muddle through life without you if our relationship should . . ."

"I don't want you to pretend that it didn't happen," Melissa returned, wanting to melt in his embrace, wanting to be lost in his love, wanting to be sure that he cared about her, but she didn't dare lose control. She didn't dare give ground until she knew where she stood with Iverson, until she knew where he stood with Nicole. What he was, what he wanted out of life, and his way of accomplishing his goals had hurt her. And his relationship with Nicole still puzzled her.

Deliberately shrugging aside any personal intimacy, struggling to keep her distance, she pushed out of his arms. "How was your week in Florida?" She felt the horrible constriction of jealousy as she thought of him and Nicole in Miami.

"Just business," he returned, shrugging.

139

"Nicole joined you."

Iverson grinned. "Not me. True, she flew down, but she was with Tom, not me."

"When were the negotiations over?" she asked, her eyes on his face.

Almost as if he understood her questions, almost as if he knew from what source her fears stemmed, Iverson said, "The negotiations in San Francisco were over yesterday, but I stayed over to help Dad on another account for his firm. I was going to surprise you today, but you left early. By the time I got to the office, you were already gone."

Melissa nodded. "I headed for Penny's. I was a little upset. Nicole called me from the airport in Miami."

"And?"

"She said you went back to Florida so you could fly back home with her." She turned away from him.

"And you thought I was again at her heels, trying to protect my contract with Dillson and Whitman?"

"Knowing how badly you want the contract, I wondered," she admitted.

"Melissa, please trust me, and don't let Nicole come between us," he said, keeping his voice low, tormenting her with his nearness, with his touch, with the soft melody of his voice.

Melissa turned her head, looking at that beloved profile, loving and cherishing the rock-hewn sturdiness that it projected, smiling at that indomitable thrust of his jaw and chin. "It's not I who is putting Nicole between us. You're the one who continually jumps at her every command. And she seems to be everywhere that you are." She crossed her hands over her chest, digging her fingers into the softness of her upper arms.

"Don't exclude me from your life," Iverson said, moving closer to her. "I can accept whatever terms you dictate. If you tell me that I can see only those

140

beautiful golden-brown eyes, that will be enough for me. Or if I can only hold your hand, that will be enough." He stopped and smiled. "But I don't think it will be enough for either of us. I'm hoping—I'm praying—that it won't."

Melissa closed her eyes, and she tried to still the erratic beating of her heart; she tried to keep the tremors out of her voice. "Can't you understand, Iverson?" A cry of anguish erupted from her heart. "I could lust with anyone else, but not you. You mean too much to me. I don't want to share you with someone else. I can't."

Iverson chuckled. "Melissa, lusting with you is perhaps the most beautiful experience that I've ever had." He lifted his right hand and again ran his fingers down her cheeks. "I miss our being together. I sort of had the feeling that we had shared ourselves and were on the road to finding love."

"A person neither finds or falls in love," she told him, her hand closing over his, stopping the tormenting motions. "Love is born between two people, and it continues to grow as long as they cherish it, as long as they nurture it."

"I think then"—Iverson slowly turned his hand, capturing Melissa's in his, gently squeezing it—"that we've given birth."

Although her soul quivered from the verbal love strokes, and her body trembled from the touch of his warm hand, Melissa would have pulled her hand from his grasp if he had turned it loose. But he clung to her, hoping to convince her of his sincerity.

"I'm just asking for a chance to cultivate this love that you're talking about, Melissa. You're not being fair to either one of us. You're denying both of us the opportunity to see if we can have love. You can't let

141

Nicole and all her lies prevent us from being together."

Finally Melissa withdrew her hand from his clasp and walked into the kitchen area, where she put on a pot of coffee. Iverson rounded the counter and stood, leaning his shoulder against the spindle columns, folding his hands over his chest.

"My caring for you is too risky," she said, her back to him. "I'm not sure what your priorities are—or who they are."

Then he was behind her, so close that he could have touched her, but he didn't. "I've been thinking about what you said to me last Sunday." He wanted to take her in his arms, to love her doubts away, but he knew that would be only a temporary solution.

"My company is very important to me, Melissa, and perhaps since my divorce from Nicole I have made it even more important. I think maybe last Sunday you made me see myself in a light that I had refused to turn on before." He caught her hand in his, gently guiding her to the breakfast table. He pulled the chair from the table and sat her down first; then he sat down across from her. "I began to equate my self-worth with what I accomplished through the Gerrick Corporation; therefore, to be worthy, I had to move constantly to greater and ever greater heights. To do this I completely broke all social ties, burying myself in work, losing touch with people. I forgot the humanness of people."

Melissa's resistance began to melt, and it dripped compassion into her soul for her mountain man. She wanted to take him in her arms, to console him, to comfort him, and to convince him of her love. She hated Nicole for having taken all his love and for having left him empty and destitute. She reached across the table and wrapped her hands around his.

"Iverson," Melissa whispered, "don't say any more."

"I've got to, sweetheart. I've got to make you understand what you mean to me." The russet eyes were dark, with only hints of their red glinting in the fathomless depths. "Although my pushing this project through is important to me and although the Gerrick Corporation is a major concern, neither overpowers or overshadows the feelings I have for you, Melissa."

"I never felt any competition from your job," she countered, feeling a stab of guilt because she had never confessed her true position at Day's Work to Iverson. But now was not the time to tell him. She would wait until after they had reconciled their differences. Then she could tell him, and they would laugh about it together. "I'm concerned about the power Nicole seems to wield over you. Time and time again I've seen her in action. She has only to call, and immediately you react."

"She had the power to ruin this project, and I was running too scared or too careful. You choose which." He smiled. "This past week I laid the cards on the table for Tom, and I totally excluded Nicole Lambert from the negotiations. I'm no longer tiptoeing around her. Whatever Tom decides is his concern. Whatever Nicole does, I'll work around it. George and I have discussed it, and he's willing for the two of us to try it on our own—without Tom, if necessary. That's what we were doing in San Francisco, drumming up more interest."

Melissa wanted to believe him, but she had to erase a final doubt. "Whom did you go to the theater with?"

"Are you my mother confessor again?"

She nodded. "I am." He looked at her, and he waited until he heard the words. "I forgive all." Then he answered.

"I went with Miss Bromley. Can you imagine what an evening I spent? A Friday evening that I shall never forget!"

Melissa laughed, tears of happiness misting in her eyes. "And afterward you came over here to me."

"Orlaine's a pretty shrewd woman. Instead of watching the play, she watched and played me. Constantly talking to me about you." He grinned. "I've never heard her sing anyone's praises like she did yours. Said if I weren't careful, you were going to get snatched from right under my nose. And she didn't stop with that. She went on and on."

Although the scent of fresh-brewed coffee filled the room, neither was thinking about it. They were lost in each other, happily reveling in the sweet glow of discovery. Yet neither moved; they continued to sit at the table, their hands intertwined, their eyes locked together.

"I broke a promise to you last weekend," she heard him say. "May I make it up to you this weekend? May I put your heart together again?"

"What would you like to do?" she asked, closing her eyes, fantasizing all kinds of romantic scenes.

"I'd like to take you fishing."

"Fishing!" Melissa exclaimed. Her eyes opened wide, and laughter began to gurgle through her soul. This wasn't what she had expected to hear. Not at all!

CHAPTER EIGHT

"You want to take me fishing?" Melissa giggled, and Iverson solemnly nodded. "Where?"

"Cherokee."

"When?"

"Tonight."

"Are you always a spur-of-the-minute man?"

"No," he said quietly, "I've been thinking about this ever since last Sunday. I couldn't get you off my mind the entire time I was away. But instead of worrying or fretting, I made plans, as though everything were going to work out. I could hardly wait to get home to take you fishing."

Melissa threw back her head, letting the peals of laughter roll from her throat. His work, her work, both were lost for the time being. "How romantic, Iverson! No sweet nothings! No seductive scenes! No enticing promises! Just a let's-go-fishing."

"I was playing it safe," he said, standing up and moving around the table, tugging her to her feet. "I have plenty of sweet nothings for you; I've planned beautiful seductive scenes; and I have one enticing promise to make to you. Fishing is just a front."

"What kind of fishing?"

"For starters, trout," he murmured. "Rainbow and brook. Later I'm going for the biggest catch of the season, for my darling's heart."

"Restrictions or limit?" she whispered.

"Creel limit ten trout. No bait restrictions. The other limit is two hearts bound together forever."

"Instead of singing for our supper we'll fish for it." Then she asked, "How far are we from this wonderland?" She moved nearer to him, delighting when his arms curled around her body, hugging her close to his hard frame.

"About fifty miles as the crow flies."

"What if the crow is driving?"

"About five miles farther."

"And what else are we going to do while we're in Cherokee?" she asked, her face lifted to his, her breath warm on his neck and chin.

"For starters we'll see the Indian Village and Frontierland. And," he added, his eyes glowing with laughter and life, "I'll even take you to Santa's Land if you'll promise to be a good girl."

"That sounds promising," she whispered, her lips wisping up the center column of his throat. "What have you got planned for the chilly nights?"

"I'll build a blaze that you'll never forget. One that will never be equaled."

"Think we'll have time for anything else?" she whispered.

"Maybe we can work in a visit to the Mountainside Theatre and see *Unto These Hills*. Afterward we'll stop for a hamburger and soda. Then we'll have dessert."

"You're determined to have dessert, aren't you?"

"Only if you desire it." He acquiesced to her will. "Although I'm starved for a taste of you, I'll do whatever you wish. I can't get your sweetness out of my mind." He groaned. "Darling girl, you have literally haunted me. Even if I wanted to, I can't escape you."

146

He smiled persuasively. "Please say you'll go with me. Let's have this weekend together. Just the two of us."

"You're willing to spend this weekend with me even if I don't sleep with you?"

"I am," he returned, meaning what he said. His agreeing not to make love to her didn't diminish his wants or desires any, but he loved Melissa enough that his only purpose wasn't in going to bed with her. He just wanted to be with her. He wanted to hear her laughter, to see her smile, to feel the warmth of her happiness.

"Isn't it rather late for us to be starting?" she asked.

"Not really."

"What are our chances of getting a motel this time of the night?"

"Excellent." The grin continued to spread across his face.

"How about camping out?" she asked. "Along the river. That way we could hike, swim, and fish. We could use my van."

"The van?"

"My van," she replied with a cocky grin. "It's ideal for overnight camping."

"Okay," he conceded, "we'll find a campsite tomorrow. But tonight let's stay at a motel."

"Am I to assume that you'd already figured all this out and have your baggage in the car?"

Iverson shook his head. "No, I don't have my luggage in the car, but my stay in Florida was productive in more than one sense. Hoping that I could persuade you to see the sincerity of my heart, I made a reservation at a motel, determined that you would have your weekend." He lifted his arms from around her. "You go get dressed and pack your bags, and we'll go by my house and get my things. Then we'll be on the road, headed for Cherokee."

She looked into his face. "This time there'll be no call from Nicole to mess things up?"

"I can't guarantee that there won't be a call from Nicole, but no one's going to mess it up, darling. I promise." He gently pushed her down the hall, swatting her bottom. "Now, hurry up and get dressed, so we can be on our way."

Laughing, Melissa raced down the hall to her bedroom, and as soon as she was out of earshot, Iverson walked to the telephone, picked it up, and dialed. When the first number didn't answer, he dialed a second number.

"Ramona, this is Iverson. Sorry to waken you so late, but I'm going to be away this weekend. I tried to reach Miss Bromley, but she didn't answer, and Dad's still in Florida. Here's a number where you can reach me, but don't call me unless it's an absolute emergency. Let Miss Bromley know as soon as you can." He listened while Ramona repeated the information. Then he replaced the receiver and sat down in one of the chairs, leafing through a magazine.

When Melissa returned with her suitcase, she was dressed in a white T-shirt that was tucked into her jeans and a long-sleeved flannel shirt that flapped loosely around her thighs. "Here I am," she announced, twirling around. "What do you think?"

"That's a leading question, lady," Iverson teased, tossing the magazine aside, and got up. He moved to where she stood and bent to grasp the handle of her suitcase in his hand. "I'll tell you when we are safely hidden away in our room at the motel, when you can't run away from me."

"It's not I who has the habit of running away," she quipped as she walked into the kitchen to scribble a note on the telephone pad for her mother. "You, Iverson Gerrick, are the one who does the running."

He raised his right hand and solemnly promised. "But I'm not running away from you again, darling. Promise."

"Are you going to leave your car here?" she asked. "If so, I'll need to tell Mom."

"No, if it's okay with you, you can follow me to the house, and we'll take the van from there."

"Fine," Melissa agreed. "What's the name of the motel?"

When he replied, she wrote the information on the pad and signed her name. "Ready," she announced, dropping the pencil on the counter.

Driving her silver and blue van, she followed him home. Before she knew it, she was waiting in the living room of the Homestead while he changed clothes and packed his bags. He came running down the stairs in a pair of jeans and a cotton shirt, his duffel bag in his hand. Dropping it at the foot of the stairs, he grabbed her hand and pulled her behind him to the storage room off the garage.

"Are you carrying one of those cane poles?" he asked as he picked up his fly rod and tackle box.

"What if I am?" she returned.

"I was thinking about loaning you one of my new fly rods, so we could have a genuine contest."

"Quite all right, old boy," she teased. "I think I can still beat you with a cane pole. Mary Jane swears by hers."

He chuckled, holding the door open with his back, letting her pass through before he switched off the light. "I'll tell you a little secret, Miss 'Lissa. Those fish on Lake Peaceful just bite when Miss Mary Jane uses that cane pole because they don't have the heart not to. That's how much they love that woman."

"We'll see," Melissa quipped. "I'll show you how

popular I am with rainbow and brook trout. Why, I'll never forget the time that Dad took me to Lake . . ."

By the time they reached the van Melissa had spun quite a tale, and Iverson asked, "Are all these stories your own?"

"You don't think I'd stoop to make up a fish story, do you?" Melissa teased, hopping into the van and flipping on the dome light. "Well, what do you think?"

"This is a beaut," he praised, his eyes running from the dash to the back. "Buy it customized like this?" She nodded. "Television, small refrigerator, sink and reservoir, bed, reclining seats, carpeted all the way." He whistled silently. "Let's go get some drinks out of the pantry, and maybe we can find some picnic supplies."

For the better part of an hour they packed the van. Pillows, covers, towels, washcloths, soap, food, and drinks. "Is this it?" Melissa asked as they tucked away the last of their foodstuffs.

"Not quite," Iverson retorted. "I need to get my luggage; then we can be on our way." As they walked into the house, he stopped at the stairs and picked up his duffel bag; then he dropped it. "Just a minute. I'll be right back. I need to let Estelle know where I'll be." He disappeared behind a swinging door, leaving Melissa alone in the living room.

While he was gone, the telephone began to ring and Melissa looked at the instrument as if it were a deadly rattler, coiled, ready to strike its victim. She listened to the unceasing clamor, each ring becoming louder and shriller. To escape she walked into the hall, picked up Iverson's bag, and carried it to the van.

By the time she returned, the ringing had stopped, and she heard Iverson's voice coming from the study. Quickly and quietly she walked across the Oriental rug to the study door just in time to hear Iverson say softly, "Nicole," and Melissa froze to the spot. Anger like she had never felt before billowed through her.

"Sorry, I can't," he said. "I have other plans." There was silence; then Melissa heard his "Yes, I'm with her." There was another long period of quiet before Iverson said, "I hadn't planned on coming back until Sunday evening. And even though it's a tough situation where she's concerned, I guess I could leave early." He laughed at something that was said. "Nothing really important. Nothing that could ever come between you and me. Just fishing."

Melissa gasped, and Iverson turned to look at her. Capping the phone, he opened his mouth to say something, but Melissa spun on her heel, walking out of the room. She didn't stop to think; she didn't wait for an explanation. All she could hear was Nicole's taunting voice; all she could hear was Nicole's laughter. Again Nicole had won. Again Iverson was running to her beck and call.

White-hot fury raged through Melissa as she slammed the front door, sped across the porch, and down the steps. She climbed into the driver's seat of her van, twisted the key, and started the ignition. Again she had let Iverson play her for a fool.

She was speeding away when Iverson came rushing out of the house, running down the drive, yelling at her, repeatedly calling her name. Through her side mirror she watched until he was nothing but a dot in a blaze of light . . . until he was nothing. She drove, not caring where she drove. Tears, furious and angry, ran unchecked down her face. For over an hour she drove through the backroads, turning from one to the other, twisting through the mountains.

The farther she drove, however, the more confused and disoriented she became and the lower her gas indicator went. Slowly her anger and humiliation gave

151

way to apprehension. So intent on her plight, anxiously trying to find her way to a main highway, she wasn't aware that a patrol car was behind her until she heard the siren and saw the twirling light behind her. Oh, my God, she breathed, fear enveloping her, paralyzing all coherent thought, blocking reason.

Reacting out of fright, she pressed the pedal to the floor and began to drive faster. She was afraid to stop, afraid because she was on a backroad by herself in the early hours of the morning. Afraid because she had no means of protecting herself. Afraid because she didn't know if it really was an officer of the law. Dear Lord, what was she going to do?

Finally the matter was taken out of her hands. Another patrol car joined the chase, pulling in front of her, blocking her way. She screeched to a jerking halt and sat behind the wheel, frozen with fright, her face white, her eyes saucers of fear. She didn't move. Even when the policeman came to her window and tapped, she refused to acknowledge him.

"Get out of the van," he commanded gruffly over and over again, the light tapping on the window changing to a harsh pounding.

Melissa stared straight ahead, never moving. She didn't even hear him. Delayed shock had set in; her fear had petrified her.

"Hey, lady, open the door!" another patrolman called from the passenger side. He began pounding on the windows, his hand curled around the butt of his pistol. "Snap out of it and open this door."

Melissa was vaguely aware that the noise had stopped, but she didn't move a muscle. She continued to stare blindly ahead of herself, seeing only the cold gray gun long after the pounding had ceased. She didn't see the two patrolmen as they walked behind the van. She didn't hear their discussion.

But she did hear that soft gravelly voice. "Melissa, open the door, darling. Unlock the door for me." Still she didn't move, but she heard him. Reassuringly Iverson called her name again and again. He coaxed her to unlock the door. Finally she turned her head and looked out the window, and she saw him.

"Iverson," she whispered. Her fright began to abate, and relief began to flow through her body. Then anger, harsh and retaliatory, began to resurge, flowing through her in undammed torrents, refusing to be stopped.

"Roll the window down, sweetheart."

His eyes were dark with worry, and his brow was creased in concern. He hadn't meant to frighten her by sending the police; he had only wanted to find her. He couldn't let her drive these mountain roads by herself. God, if anything happened to her, he'd never forgive himself.

Melissa, however, didn't see the concern that suffused his face. All she could see was his infidelity; all she could hear was his broken promise. She unlocked the door and opened it, and she jumped at Iverson, her fingers crooked, clawing at his face.

"You low-down—"

Seeing the anger in her face, hearing the fury in her words, Iverson acted quickly. He grabbed both of her hands in his, wrenching them down; then he locked her to his chest, knocking her glasses askew as he muffled the verbal torrent that spewed from her mouth like the molten lava of an erupting volcano.

"Purty feisty little cuss," the older patrolman said, walking up to them. "Want us to search the van?"

Iverson shook his head. "No, Pollard, I think I can handle it from here on."

"Recognize her?" Pollard beamed his flashlight in Melissa's face.

"Yeah," Iverson slowly drawled. "She works for me."

The patrolman laughed sardonically. "An' this is how she shows her gratitude. Burglarizing your house."

Melissa felt Iverson's chest shake with his laughter, and she tensed.

She waited for that minute when he relaxed his hold, to push out of his arms, doubling her fists pounding his chest.

"You—"

"Sure you don't want us to take her into custody, Mr. Gerrick?" The patrolman sympathized as Iverson tightened his arms around Melissa, again pressing her face into the softness of his shirt, his strength serving good purpose. He wrapped her slight form to his gigantic proportions, easily crushing her rebellion, easily muffling further outcries and maledictions. "No, I'd like to handle this myself." Forcibly keeping Melissa's head against his shoulder, he continued to talk to the patrolman. "Thanks for helping me locate her. If it's okay with you, I'll drive her and the van back home."

Pollard laughed, the sound unpleasant to Melissa's ears. "Sure you trust this little vixen, Mr. Gerrick? She don't look none too savory to me."

Melissa finally wilted in Iverson's arms, too tired to continue the battle. Then Iverson loosened his iron grip on her, and she lifted her face. Iverson was moved. His heart almost broke within his chest. Her eyes were swollen from crying, and her face was blanched of all color.

Lowering his face, his lips next to her ears, he crooned for her alone, "Oh, baby, why did you make me do it?"

But they were the wrong words. Gaining a second wind, the adrenaline flowing unchecked, Melissa took advantage of his slackened grip, and she twisted herself free, pushing her hair out of her face with one hand and jabbing at her glasses with the other. "Damn you," she hissed, backing away from him, "don't you baby me. You're the one who had the highway patrol chasing me. You're the one who frightened the life out of me."

The patrolman looked from Melissa to Iverson and back to Melissa. "Mr. Gerrick, I think you're making a mistake. This gal ain't gonna appreciate you giving her a break. Might as well let us haul her in here and now."

"Thanks, Pollard," Iverson said firmly, "but this is the way I want it."

"Okay," Pollard mumbled dubiously, walking back to his car. "Have it your own way." He opened the door and eased himself inside.

"Where are they going?" Melissa demanded, watching the other patrolmen as they retraced their steps, moving toward their car also. "Why are they leaving you here with me?"

"They're leaving because they have work to do, and they are leaving me here with you because this is where I belong."

"I'll be damned if it is!" Melissa belted out. "You started this little charade, Mr. Gerrick, so let's continue with it. I don't want to be left in your custody. I'd much rather be with them." She pointed to the idling patrol car.

"Okay." Iverson shrugged, knowing that he couldn't reason with her in her present state of mind. "You go with them, and I'll drive the van back." He moved toward the driver's seat. "Where do you want me to leave it? My house or yours?"

"Don't you dare touch my van with your filthy hands," she spat out.

Iverson leveled his gaze at her, all amusement wiped from his eyes, a sad seriousness underlying his words. "I don't think you have much of a choice, Melissa. Either I drive and you ride with me, or you'll be arrested for burglary."

"Arrested for burglary!" Melissa shrieked.

"That's right," Iverson returned. "If you don't get into the van quietly, and if you don't allow me to escort you wherever you're going, I'll press charges and have you arrested for burglary."

"But you can't prove that."

"No?" he droned, lifting a brow. "I think you've got quite a few of my possessions in the back of your van, and the police will believe me before you." He smiled sardonically. "What do you want, Melissa? It's your choice."

She shrugged, giving up a second time. "Once again you've given me no choice but your choice. What can I do?"

"Whatever you want," he returned, sweet gentleness coating his words.

Melissa wiped her hands down the legs of her jeans, and she spun on her heel, walking to the side of the van. Rather than getting in the passenger's seat, however, she moved to the back, yanking her glasses off and putting them on the shelf behind the seat. Then she lay down. She heard Iverson slam the side door and lock it; she heard the patrol car as it drove off. Then she felt the van sway with Iverson's weight as he made his way to where she lay. She heard the low click as he turned on one of the dome lights.

"Melissa, will you listen to me?" he asked, sitting on the side of the seat, his hands touching her shoulders.

She flinched away from him. "You've got what you wanted. Leave me alone."

He slowly pulled his hand back, and he sat staring

156

at her, feeling her anger, her anguish, her embarrassment. And he hurt for her and with her; truly they were one in her pain and suffering. "I had to find you, sweetheart. I was worried sick. I didn't know what would happen to you. You're not familiar with these roads or these driving conditions."

"So you sent the North Carolina highway patrol after me," she ranted. "You told them that I stole—"

Her outcry was more than Iverson could stand. He couldn't keep his hands off her any longer. He had to hold her close; he had to convince her of his concern. Lying on the seat by her, he stretched his body beside hers, curving his big frame around her small, angry one, and he laid his hand on her shoulder.

"I had to tell them that to get them to search for you, darling. I didn't think about their frightening you. I was too worried to do much thinking. I could see you stranded out here. Even worse, I could see you careening over the side of the mountain on some of these narrow backroads. I was desperate."

"And I was desperate too," she exploded, flipping over. "I was scared to death. I didn't know what they were going to do to me. I didn't even know if they were policemen or not. And—and"—she looked into those beautiful eyes that were shaded from the soft dome light—"and when one of them waved that gun in my face—" She stopped, inhaled deeply, and exclaimed heatedly. "He waved a gun in my face, Iverson!"

"Hush, darling," Iverson cooed, trying not to laugh at her outrage, understanding her fear. "Everything's all right. I'm here with you." They lay together, wrapped in each other's arms. Then Melissa saw the humor in the situation, and she began to laugh softly, her body shaking against Iverson's. Sure that her fear

157

had dissipated, he whispered, "Are you ready to apologize to me now?"

"Apologize to you?" she murmured, pulling out of his arms, lifting her hands and brushing her hair from her face.

"For not trusting me."

"For not trusting you?"

"Must you repeat everything I say?" he teased gently.

"What—what are you talking about?" she asked.

"You walked into the study, and I presume overheard me talking on the phone. Then without giving me a hearing, without giving me a chance to tell you about the call, you ran out of the house and drove away."

"I overheard you talking with Nicole," Melissa confessed, "and I was livid with anger. I just didn't think beyond that moment. All I could hear was you calling Nicole's name; all I could see was your broken promise, your broken word."

"Will you never trust me?"

Melissa lifted her eyes and gazed into the shadowed face of the man she loved. "Yes," she whispered, "I trust you, and I'm sorry that I left. I'm sorry that I frightened you."

"Would you mind so desperately if we returned to Asheville earlier on Sunday than we had originally planned?" He asked the question before he gave his explanation. Patiently he waited for her answer.

"I'll mind," she replied, "but I know you wouldn't ask if it wasn't important." She hesitated, then said, "And I know by your asking that it is a very important request."

"It is, my precious," he said in a husky voice, pulling her even closer to him, banding her to him with

158

manacles of love, promising himself that he would never let her go. "Orlaine called to tell—"

Melissa's fingers stopped their ministrations of love, and she tensed. "Orlaine . . . Orlaine was the one you were talking to." She laughed, murmuring joyously, "You were talking with Miss Bromley!"

He chuckled softly with her, glad that she could see the humor behind the ghastly evening. "I was talking with Miss Bromley. She must have had a premonition that I had gone to your house because she asked if you were with me. Then she jokingly asked if I had anything important planned for this weekend."

"That's when you told her nothing but fishing!" Melissa laughed at her own foolishness.

"And she said if it were nothing more important than fishing, she would like to have our illustrious presence at dinner Sunday evening. She wondered if we could come early for that."

"Oh, Iverson," Melissa said contritely, "please forgive me. I didn't know."

"No, darling, you didn't know," he whispered, planting soft kisses on her forehead, silently adding, *I just wish you trusted me enough to have waited for an explanation. I wish I were more sure of your trust and confidence in me.*

"When I heard you repeat Nicole's name, I just assumed . . ." she began tentatively, hoping he'd accept her explanation.

"I know."

"Forgive me," she whispered, lifting her mouth to his.

"Forgiven," he declared, adding, "Forgive me?" His lips touched hers, sealing their penitent confessions with a kiss.

"Forgiven," came her muffled cry, her words mingling into the essence of their caress.

Later both of them scampered to the front of the van and because Iverson knew where they were going, he drove. They didn't need to go to the motel now since it was daylight by the time they got to their destination. They selected their campsite and although they hadn't slept, they drove into town after a brief nap, stopping at a restaurant for breakfast. Afterward they began their exploration of Cherokee, laughing and talking, whiling their morning away. They ambled through the novelty and gift shops; they visited the craft shops. And in one shop they munched on hot cookies and sipped a cup of fresh coffee while they browsed through the assorted kitchen items. Then they slowly meandered through the Fort Tomahawk Mini-Mall, going from one boutique to the next.

In one of the shops that specialized in lingerie, Melissa spied a beautiful yellow nightgown and peignoir, but she wouldn't buy it for herself because it was too expensive. Iverson saw the longing in her eyes and watched as she touched the material.

Moving close to her, he asked softly so that the salesclerk couldn't overhear, "Would you accept it if I bought it for you?"

Melissa dropped her head, letting her hair fall forward to hide her face. "I don't think so. I've—I've never accepted intimate gifts like this from a . . . from any . . . man before."

He rubbed the yellow gossamer material through his fingers gently, looking at it rather than at her. "I'm not just any man, Melissa, and I'm not buying it for an ulterior reason. It's beautiful, and it will look lovely on you. I'd like for you to have it."

"So I can wear it for you?" she whispered.

"Only if you wish to wear it for me," he returned, refusing to rise to the bait. "If you don't, I still want to buy it for you." He dropped the material, lifted his

160

hand to her face, and tucked his fingers under her chin, raising her eyes to his. "I want to buy this for you because I like you. I'm not expecting any repayment." His voice hardened. "I wouldn't accept repayment. I'll accept no less than yourself, freely given."

Melissa smiled, wrapping her hand around his. "Please buy it for me, Iverson."

Then they meandered into the sandwich shop, buying themselves a light lunch, spending the early part of their afternoon in the Oconaluftee Indian Village and the Cherokee Botanical Garden; the latter portion of the day they spent at their campsite, hiking on the nature trails, resting at the falls. Here they sat in the quiet of the forest and watched the panorama of nature as it unfolded just for them. They sat close together, and they held hands, loving without making love, discovering each other, freely sharing, freely giving.

That night they dressed casually in shirts and jeans and drove into town to the Mountainside Theatre to see the outdoor drama, *Unto These Hills*. As the chill of the evening settled on them, Iverson put his arm around Melissa and pulled her closer to the warmth of his chest and shoulders. And together they followed the story of the Cherokee Indian from the arrival of DeSoto in 1540 through their tragic removal to the west over the trail of tears.

Melissa laughed with them, and during the removal scene, she cried with them as the words of "Amazing Grace," sung in the Cherokee language, wafted through the mountainside amphitheater. Melissa felt the Cherokee's tragedy and when the performance was over, she clapped, unashamed of the tears that sparkled in her eyes. The Cherokees had survived, and they, the first Americans, were still an important part of modern American culture; they were still a unique and distinct part of the mountain culture. And while they were saving their heritage for Americans of tomorrow, they were sharing their heritage with Americans of today.

"That was beautiful," she said as she and Iverson sat in a local restaurant eating hamburgers and fries and drinking sodas.

They sat for a long time talking about the performance before they drove back to their campsite and parked. After they got out they held hands and walked beside the swirling water of the river. They didn't talk, yet neither found the silence cumbersome or uncomfortable. They were discovering each other, slowly unraveling personalities. Eventually they returned to the van.

"Are you sure?" Iverson asked.

"I'm sure," she replied, opening the door herself, getting in.

Iverson followed her in and they sat on the backseat, locked away from the world, wrapped safely and securely in each other's arms, looking at the deciduous forest that was sprayed silver from the moon above. The breathtaking beauty of the night scene caused Melissa to shiver, and she cuddled closer to Iverson—her strength, her mountain.

"Cold," he whispered.

"Yes," she murmured. "I think we need that fire you were describing to me." Her voice dropped until it was a faint softness. "I suppose we should have stayed in the motel as you wanted. It's going to be rather difficult to build a fire in the van."

"Not nearly as difficult as you would think," Iverson whispered, his lips trailing up the slender line of her neck.

Slowly she turned her face, her soft cheek brushing

162

against his lips, and her faint touch, like the stroke of a match, ignited Iverson's ardor, setting him ablaze.

They quickly lowered the seat, making their bed, fumbling with the sheet, the pillows, and the cover. They undressed, and then lay down, hidden beyond the silvery rays of moonlight that wafted through the windshield. Neither gave a thought to the soft, flowing yellow gown that lay neglected in its bed of tissue on the front seat of the van.

Kneeling over her, Iverson's lips began a slow and thorough investigation of her face—her lips, her eyes, her ears, the tip of her nose; then he touched the central column of her neck, his lips moving down to her full breasts that peaked pertly, inviting his caress. He left butterfly-soft kisses all around the gentle mounds, but he never touched the sensitive tips.

His hands, joining in the pleasurable quest, began to glide tantalizingly over her stomach, over her thighs, and up again. Then he lightly ran his fingers over her navel, barely touching her, teasing her, tormenting her. His fingers touched just enough to leave her burning for more.

"That feels so good," she mumbled incoherently, her voice thick and husky with wanting. "Please, don't stop, Iverson."

She arched her back, trying desperately to thrust her breast in his mouth, but again he evaded the provocative flesh, whetting her desire to the point of total abandon. His mouth strayed farther down her midriff to stroke the tender flesh around her navel, his hand moving, warmly touching the downy-soft opening.

"Melissa." He sighed, his breath oozing like hot, thick honey over her skin. "I can never get enough of you, my darling. You're my day; you're my night."

Melissa's hand ran across his chest, across his rippled muscles, down his stomach, lightly touching, repaying him torment for torment, delighting when his great body began to quiver for more. She tenderly stroked him, reveling in his sighs of contentment, his pleasure becoming her pleasure. She moved her hand; she twisted; she pushed him on his back.

Now it was her mouth and her hands that were loving him, creating a heat wave from which there would be no survivors. Yet Melissa had no fears; she completely trusted Iverson. No matter what the future held; they loved each other, and their love would make way for whatever came. She would protect him with her love; and he would protect her with his.

When she went to pull him on top of her, he turned her on her side so that her buttocks were cradled in the cup of his stomach and thighs. Gently his big hands stroked the rounded curves, every now and then slipping between her legs, dancing up and down her thighs. Keeping her on her side, he eased one of his legs between hers, spreading her thighs apart, and his left hand moved under her body, stimulating her desires.

His stomach to her back, he slid down on the bed and raised her leg with his. He pulled her closer against his chest and stomach, his right hand touching and caressing her. She soon found herself moving with him in that primitive age-old dance of love.

She arched her body, giving herself in total abandon, becoming a part of the mountain wilderness, loving her man, letting him love her. She closed her eyes, running her tongue over her lips, moistening them as she purred in wanton abandonment. She closed one hand over Iverson's, pressing his palm into the softness of her breasts, and she reached behind herself, cupping his flexed buttocks with her other hand.

They moved together. Each selfishly took; each unselfishly gave. Both sighed their pleasure. They moaned their heated endearments, each groaned encouragement, and both cried out in ecstasy when their deep-seated hunger was assuaged, when she and Iverson become one in body, soul, and spirit.

Although the evening was chilly, Melissa's body was covered with a fine sheen of perspiration that reflected the silvery web of moonlight. She had scaled her mountain, and now she wilted beside her love, her eyes closed, her breathing deep and erratic. Gently Iverson turned her on her back, and his lips began to thank her for the completeness of her giving.

He softly kissed her face. He gently rubbed his hand slowly down her legs and slowly up her legs.

"Melissa, I know the words are old and shopworn, but I can't think of any that express the way I feel but them." He paused; then said from the depth of his soul, "I love you."

Melissa twined her fingers in the thick russet hair, her fingers digging into his scalp. Though her answer was soft, it was loud enough for Iverson to hear. "And I love you, my darling."

"Now that we've said that"—Iverson laughed, his warm breath splaying across the tenderly sensitive flesh of her tummy—"let's get to the harder part of this personal involvement."

"I didn't realize that it could get any harder." Melissa giggled.

Iverson playfully swatted her hip. "Naughty girl. You're distracting me."

"I don't mind," she whispered.

"Right now, I do," he retorted. "I've got important matters to discuss with you."

"That being?"

"That being, Ms. Phillips, will you marry me?"

"You couldn't have put it any better, Mr. Gerrick," she said, smiling. "I most certainly will."

Iverson got up, crawled over her, and rummaged through the baggage. Melissa, pulling the sheet over her, rolled on her side and watched curiously as he dug through the fishing gear, through the clothes, to the small bag that lay underneath the heap. Finally he looked up at her and grinned, holding a bottle of wine in the air.

"The better to celebrate with, my dear."

Melissa laughed, feeling elated.

He grinned at her, holding his arm out. "Shall we drink to our engagement, Ms. Phillips?"

Then Melissa remembered her nightgown and negligee. "Just a minute. I can't drink to my engagement unless I'm formally dressed." She threw the sheet aside and dashed to the front of the van, tenderly lifting the white tissue paper, carefully unwrapping her gift. Taking off the price tags, she stood, stretching her naked body. She lifted her hands above her head and dropped the glimmering material over her head, letting it glide down her body. "Now," she said, returning to the bed, "I'm properly attired, and I'm ready to drink to our engagement."

She twined her arm through his and bound together they sipped their wine and commemorated their love. Afterward they talked; they laughed; and they made love again. Then they snuggled under the sheet and blanket, Melissa laying her head on Iverson's shoulder, Iverson folding his arm around her.

"We'll announce our engagement at Orlaine's dinner tomorrow night. Okay?"

"Um-hm," she agreed contentedly.

"Will your family be back in time for dinner?"

Melissa laughed. "They aren't supposed to be home until tomorrow, but if I know Charlie Blake, he'll hustle them to the car and drive straight home tonight. Claims he can't sleep in any bed but his own."

"We'll call in the morning," Iverson said. "And we'll tell both our families together." He paused, then asked, "How many are there in your family?"

"Mom, my stepsister, Penny, her husband, Charlie, and their two sons, Randal and Lane. You don't think that's too many for us to invite to dinner at Miss Bromley's, do you?"

Iverson laughed. "Hardly. Orlaine loves to entertain, and she will delight in being asked to cook our engagement dinner."

"The question is, however, will she mind our inviting so many to a dinner that she's going to prepare?"

"And the answer is the same. Orlaine will be delighted that we chose her to do it."

"Will your dad be there?"

He nodded his head. "Orlaine's picking him up at the airport in the morning."

"What about your brother and sister?"

"They won't be able to come on such short notice, but we'll call them, so I can introduce you to them."

"I'll call Dad and my stepmother, Thekla, in the morning," she whispered, feeling a certain sadness because they wouldn't be with her when she and Iverson made the announcement.

"You can tell them that we'll be coming to Texas very soon so they can meet me in person," Iverson consoled her gently, sensing her sorrow.

"Thank you, my darling." She sighed, lapsing into a contented quietness, thinking about herself and Iverson, warming herself in the flames of their love.

She felt so wanted and so cherished, that feeling that comes from the security of knowing beyond any shadow of a doubt that you are protected by the strength of love. Now she felt that security; she had her rugged mountain man who was hewn from this rocky terrain. He's rugged and indomitable, she would

167

be the first to concede. Hard and unyielding, she would also concur. But offsetting these qualities was that vein of gold that ran through his toughness, that special wealth that he possessed—tenderness, gentleness, caring, and loving.

She had so much she needed to tell him, so much that she wanted to tell him, but tonight wasn't the time. Tomorrow, she promised herself. Tomorrow as they fished she would tell him the truth about her position at Day's Work. Yawning, she burrowed and snuggled into the warmth of Iverson Gerrick, sliding into the tranquility of deep sleep.

CHAPTER NINE

Waking early the next morning, Iverson and Melissa laughed and talked, conspiring their surprise together. Dressing hastily, they drove to town and from a pay phone began to make their calls, the first one being to Orlaine Bromley.

"Orlaine," Iverson said, "would you mind if we invite Melissa's family over for dinner also?"

"Does this mean what I think it means?" she asked.

Iverson chuckled, winking at Melissa. "Don't go playing matchmaker, Miss Bromley. Just answer the question."

"We're not at the Gerrick Corporation this morning," Orlaine countered crisply. "I'm in my home on my own territory. And if you want me to slave over a hot stove all day to entertain your friends, then you'll tell me exactly what I want to know."

Iverson threw back his head and laughed. "Miss Bromley, even if we were discussing the Gerrick Corporation, you'd act just like this. I don't know of one person who intimidates you."

"That's better," Orlaine said. "Now, tell me what all this means."

"I just want the opportunity to get to know her family a little bit better," Iverson replied. "And this seemed to be a good opportunity. Of course"—he looked over the receiver at Melissa and both of them grinned—"you can never tell where it may go from there."

"Iverson," Orlaine declared in her booming voice, "I would be delighted to entertain the entire state of North Carolina if I thought it would bring you happiness."

Iverson's eyes rested warmly on Melissa, and he said softly, "I am very happy, Orlaine. Probably happier than I have ever been in my entire life. I'm glad you talked me into going to the theater with you last night."

"What time shall I expect you?" she asked.

"What time do you prefer?"

"Well, to be frank," Orlaine returned, "I'd like us to have a very informal gathering, so your dad and I can get to know them too." She added, "I wouldn't mind them dropping in about four or five this afternoon. Give us plenty of time to meet and get to know one another."

"Melissa and I will be delighted to see you about four or five."

"Good," Orlaine concluded curtly, her mind already on the dinner. "I can hardly wait."

Next they called Melissa's mother, who was home, then Penny and Charlie, and although the invitation was on the spur of the moment, no one refused. All suspected something, but not one guessed the enormity of the dinner. They had an idea that Iverson and Melissa were getting serious; they just had no idea how serious.

After they had made their phone calls and were eating breakfast, Melissa tried to broach the subject of Day's Work to Iverson. She wanted to explain to him before he met her mother, but Iverson, so caught up in wedding plans, shoved it aside. "Not now, sweetheart. We promised not to talk about work." He added, smiling, "I've got something important to tell you also, but we'll talk about it later. Right now let's enjoy our day."

"Okay," Melissa replied, "but promise me we'll talk tonight, Iverson. No later."

"Tonight," he assured her. "Now, let's go fishing."

Although they spent the morning by the river, they didn't seriously address the subject of fishing, and a little after noon they packed the van and headed for Asheville. Again Melissa tried to tell Iverson about Linda and Day's Work, but he pushed the subject aside, promising her that they would discuss it later.

Deciding to dismiss it until he introduced the topic himself, Melissa sat back and enjoyed the ride home. After they got their clothes, they rode directly to Orlaine's and dressed for the evening. Melissa deliberately chose the romantic look again, wearing another outfit Thekla had given her. The matching blouse and skirt were made of soft beige lace and had an old-fashioned charm and beauty, which fitted Melissa's romantic mood perfectly. The pearl buttons down the front and the leg-of-mutton sleeves made it ultimately feminine, and the stand-up collar with its ruffled border accented her smiling face. The skirt, scalloped at the bottom and loosely gathered, was cinched at the waist with a wide lace sash.

Her only accessories were her grandmother Bowman's tiny pearl earrings and brooch, each of which was encased in gold filigree, and to give herself added height, Melissa wore a pair of cobra-skin heels that were the same soft shade of beige as the blouse and skirt. Miss Bromley offered to comb her hair, and Melissa had willingly acquiesced. When Orlaine was through, a chignon of curls crowned a full, windblown Gibson girl, and sun-kissed brown bangs gently fanned across Melissa's forehead to enhance her golden-honey

171

eyes and to frame her face. While they were together Orlaine confided in Melissa that she was planning to retire and marry Iverson's father. Iverson knew about this, and couldn't have been happier. The announcement would be made soon, but she wanted to tell Melissa.

Although Melissa wanted to share *her* news with Orlaine, she and Iverson kept their secret through the meal, touching hands every once in a while, frequently brushing their legs together under the table, smiling furtively at each other. The others at the table watched them with amusement, taking great pleasure in the newness and beauty of the two lovers. Then Iverson stood up and walked into the kitchen, returning with a chilled bottle of apple cider and clean glasses.

As he set the wineglasses down beside each plate, he said, "Even you, Randal and Lane, can join in our celebration." He poured their glasses full of the sparkling, bubbly drink. Then he straightened and held one arm out, his fingers curled around the stem of the glass; the other arm he put around Melissa's shoulders, drawing her firmly to his side.

"And now, ladies and gentlemen"—he smiled at the twitter of laughter, amused at the undercurrent of suspense he was building—"I will tell you the purpose of this grand family gathering." He planted a kiss on Melissa's cheek and winked at the boys, who were giggling. "Melissa June Phillips and I, Iverson Bradley Gerrick, are going to be married."

"To Iverson and Melissa," Orlaine cheered. "I think it's marvelous."

"Married," Linda exclaimed, stunned. "You're going to marry him!" She shook her head a moment and pondered, finally asking, "When did you start liking him, Melissa? I thought you hated him Friday evening."

"I don't think she ever liked me, Mrs. Cresswell." Iverson laughed. "She moved directly from hate to marriage, falling in love with me on the way."

"I must agree with you, Iverson. Melissa never liked you. However, I must disagree with the rest of your statement. Love you, she may, but she didn't fall into it. Not my Melissa." She smiled her blessing on her daughter. "I, too, offer my congratulations, and I lift my glass to you." She winked and added teasingly, "To a job well done and to a day's work."

Melissa's cheeks flamed red, and she glanced at Iverson to see if he had heard her mother's remark. Apparently not, she thought, relief seeping through her body. And even if he had, he wouldn't have known that Linda was speaking about his endorsement for Day's Work.

The warm wishes of joy and happiness continued, everyone talking at once, questions asked and answered, the whys and the hows explained. Dinner over, the toast drunk, the group migrated to the living room and bunched around the fire. As the evening darkened, Orlaine lit the oil lamps that sat on either end of the mantelpiece, and the flickering light from the lamps and the fireplace danced shadows on those assembled. Expectantly they waited for the answer to their last question.

Iverson sat in one of the massive rockers, and Melissa knelt at his feet, her head on his thigh, one arm draped over his lap. He was explaining that they were going to be married as soon as Melissa would set the date. He smiled down at her, running his hands through her hair. "It can't be too soon for me."

"Oh, Melissa," Penny squealed, "I always knew that some guy would come along, sweep you off your

173

feet, and make you give up that idea of being a dedicated career woman the rest of your life. Now you can give up Day's—" She noticed the stricken look that whitened Melissa's countenance, and she hesitated. She stammered, "You can—you can give up your job with Day's Work and be a dedicated wife and mother like me. Can't she, Charlie?"

Melissa slowly breathed a sigh of relief, glad that Penny had caught herself. "While I plan to be a dedicated wife and mother, Penny, I still plan to have a career. I don't know that I'm cut out to stay around the house all day."

"Are you taking this sitting down, Iverson?" Charlie joked innocently.

"Well," Iverson drawled, still contemplating Linda's unusual toast to Melissa, "I'm not about to tangle with Melissa right now in front of everybody. If I've learned anything during the past two months, I've learned that she's a fighter, and she doesn't take anything sitting down." He paused and added, "Or standing up, for that matter."

Although the others laughed, Melissa heard the hesitancy in Iverson's remark, and she alone understood that he didn't intend to let the comment lie. As he said, he wouldn't discuss it with her in front of the others, but he planned to discuss it later in private.

When the boys began to lie down on the rug Penny realized that it was time for them to leave.

Although Orlaine offered to let the boys sleep upstairs, Penny insisted on leaving.

Orlaine then turned to Melissa, saying, "Their wraps are upstairs in the guest bedroom closet, Melissa. Will you get them for me, please?"

Melissa, jumping to her feet, scurried to the bedroom that Orlaine had indicated, and she rummaged through the closet, pulling out jackets and sweaters.

174

She heard the door quietly close behind her, and over her shoulder she saw Iverson leaning against it. "You can take your time because the boys are already asleep, so everyone is relaxing."

"Come help me," she said, "my arms are full."

Iverson walked toward her, but he didn't shut the closet door. Rather, he began to unload her arms, dropping jackets and sweaters to the floor at their feet, moving himself into the warm cubicle provided by her extended arms. "This is where I need to be."

"Mmm," Melissa murmured lovingly. "I'd much rather hold you in my arms than those."

"Good," Iverson whispered, his head lowering as her face lifted, their lips meeting in a sweet and quick kiss. "I'm ready to leave this place and all this company. I'd like to find us a place for ourselves. What about you?"

"Me too." She sighed, her arms around his back, her hands curled on his shoulders. "Where do you think that place will be?"

"How about staying with me tonight?" he suggested, taking her glasses off and tossing them gently on the bed so he could place kisses over her face.

"Sounds good," she agreed, quickly tiring of the nipping pecks, moving her face, her lips seeking his.

"And we can ride to work together in the morning," he said, his mouth searching leisurely for her mouth.

"Umm, that sounds good," she returned, her words muffled into silence as his lips landed on hers in a long kiss. When he finally lifted his face, Melissa pulled away and said, "Orlaine told me her news. She plans to retire and marry your father."

"She let the cat out of the bag. I wanted to tell you later."

"When is she leaving?"

"The end of next month."

"That soon!" Melissa exclaimed, then asked, "Who's going to take her place?"

"Jarvis."

"But he's your assistant."

"He *was* my assistant. When he comes back I plan to promote him."

"Who's going to be your new assistant?"

"Who else?" His eyes twinkled. "My temporary assistant seems qualified to me."

"I—I can't," Melissa whispered, shocked with the turn of the conversation.

"Of course you can, darling," Iverson told her. "I don't think the Gerrick Corporation can do without you now." His voice lowered to a seductive level. "I know I can't. I want you beside me all the time, day and night."

"The Gerrick Corporation will do just fine without me," Melissa replied cautiously. Tingles of fear ran up her back. How possessive he sounded. Just like Les! "But Day's Work would be more than happy to send you an excellent replacement for the position."

"I don't want anyone else," he told her, "I want you. When I went into the office Friday I began the paperwork. All I need to do is contact Day's Work, so I can pick up your fee. And you'll be free of that dinky agency."

Melissa stared at him. She couldn't believe what he said. Finally she swallowed the huge lump in her throat, and she began to shake her head slowly from side to side. "I'm flattered that you want me, but I'm sorry, I can't do it." She remembered those last months at SeaCo when she had worked so closely with Les. She wouldn't go through that again.

"Of course you can. I'm counting on you."

"You should have asked me first."

"Why? You can handle the job."

"That's not it," she returned. "I know I can handle the job. It's just that I already have a job."

"Honey, I don't want you to waste your time with Day's Work. You'll never go any place with that little hole-in-the-wall employment agency. Whereas, if you work for the Gerrick Corporation, you'll be paid for your knowledge and expertise."

"But I'm happy where I am." She smiled. "And I happen to be the manager of that little hole-in-the-wall employment agency! And I'm about to be made a partner!"

Iverson's hands dropped from her, and he stepped back. He didn't laugh at her little joke. "You manage Day's Work?"

His words were emotionless. They were the eye of the storm, the calm before all hell broke loose. He couldn't believe it. How could fate have been so unkind to him? First he had fallen in love with Nicole, who had been wrapped up in her career—and her father's business. Now Melissa.

"You and Ms. Bowman will be partners?" His voice was still quiet but louder. He moved around the room, sliding his hands into his pockets.

Melissa nodded. "Ms. Bowman and I will be more than partners; we're mother and daughter."

"Mrs. Cresswell—" His face again was a mirror of confusion.

Melissa picked up her glasses and put them back on. "Mrs. Cresswell is my mother. For business purposes she uses her maiden name, Bowman."

Iverson was dumbfounded, and he stared at her. "Why did you wait so long to tell me?" Again she made the attempt to reply, but Iverson didn't let her speak. "You never told me that your mother was the owner of Day's Work." Anger began to replace his confusion, and it swept through him in tidal-wave proportions. "Why didn't you tell me this when you applied for this position?" he asked, hunching his shoulders.

"Because you wouldn't have hired me at the time. You were adamantly opposed to Day's Work and to the owner in particular. In your frame of mind you wouldn't have considered hiring me. I was the Texan you spoke to on the phone the Friday before I reported to work. And, remember, you explicitly told me not to come." Taking a short breath but continuing to speak before he had a chance to break in, she said, "I didn't tell you because I wanted a chance to prove that you were wrong about Day's Work."

Iverson laughed, the sound curt and mocking. "You wanted my endorsement pretty badly, didn't you?"

"I never made any secret of wanting it. That was my primary purpose in taking the job."

"No matter what means you had to employ, Melissa?"

"Of course it mattered what means I had to employ. I knew that I was qualified for the job, and I knew that given the chance I could prove it to you. I didn't do anything underhanded or wrong."

"You haven't done anything wrong? You deceived me. All this time, your main concern has been your agency, hasn't it? Not really me?" His face had hardened, and the angular lines looked as if they were sculpted from granite. "Is that what Linda meant, Melissa, when she toasted you on a job well done?"

"She was joking, Iverson, and she didn't mean anything by it."

"Looks like I'm not the only one who will do anything to get a deal through."

"When I took this assignment," Melissa reminded him gently, "I didn't know you, and I had no intention of falling in love with you, certainly no intention of

attracting you as a way of getting the endorsement."
She smiled. "And certainly it didn't matter whom you
got as an employee as long as you hired a competent
one, did it?"

He shrugged, never giving an inch. "I don't like
having been deceived." He walked to the window and
ran his fingers through the thick gathering of ruffles on
the curtains.

"You weren't deceived. If we hadn't begun to love
each other, you wouldn't have found out about me. I
would have worked for you, and when the contract
ended, I would have walked away, and you wouldn't
have seen me again."

"I wonder, do you love me or just profess to love
me?"

"I love you. But I'm not going to let your fears
cause me to give up my job or to take a job with your
firm. I'll probably give up work entirely when we start
our family, but until then I'll choose my own career."

"I don't mind you working," Iverson returned.
"But why not at the Gerrick Corporation? Why must
it be with Day's Work?"

Melissa walked to the foot of the bed and stooped
down, picking up the jackets and sweaters. "Why
must it be the Gerrick Corporation and not Day's
Work?" she countered.

"Because you would be involved with me and my
company," Iverson answered. "Wherever I went you
could go. We'd be together."

"As cruel as this is going to sound, Iverson," Melissa said, "that's one of the reasons why I don't want
to come to the Gerrick Corporation." She felt Iverson's penetrating gaze on her, but she wouldn't look
up. She found it difficult enough to talk about Les
without looking into Iverson's hard and unyielding
face. "Les Strader was the executive whom I worked

179

for at SeaCo. We started going together after I was promoted to his assistant. At first it was wonderful; we enjoyed being with each other. I thought what we had might develop into love, but the longer we dated, the more possessive Les became and the more I knew I didn't want his kind of love. I had no time for myself." She drew a deep breath and flexed her shoulders, trying to fight off the suffocating feeling that enshrouded her as she remembered those last months working under Les.

"What happened?" Iverson asked.

"I eventually broke up with him, and the tension was unbearable. He wouldn't believe it was over. He began a subtle form of harassment."

"And you think it'll be the same with us?" Iverson asked, a hard ring to the tone. "You don't want to spend your time with me? You think if you spend too much time around me that our love will die?"

Melissa shook her head, denying his allegations. "I didn't love Les, but I love you, Iverson. Just like you, however, I have fears. And although I know that I won't ruin our love by coming to work full-time at the Gerrick Corporation, I don't want to. Mother made me manager of Day's Work, and as soon as I go back there full-time, she's going to make me a legal owner."

He sighed his resignation. "Would you stay with me until I can get a replacement?"

"No," Melissa answered. "I think it would be better if I didn't; however, I have several applicants who would qualify for the job. May I send them out for an interview?"

"I'm just not sure about hiring any of your employees," he replied. "The ones you sent out before were—well . . ." He left the sentence hanging, shrugging his shoulders dismissively.

"I haven't proven anything to you, have I?"

He smiled. "You've proven to me that you're a very talented and capable young woman and quite resourceful, too, but I haven't changed my mind about those other women whom you've sent out." His voice was hard and firm. "I wouldn't have one of them working in my office."

"Yet you tolerate incompetence every day," Melissa said. "Have you never stopped to wonder why so many women failed to meet your standards? Have you never wondered why?" Before he could interrupt her, she began to list the many grievances she had against Ramona.

"All those things may be true," he admitted, giving her the benefit of the doubt, reverting to the hardnosed executive whom Melissa knew so well. "But the women whom you sent were incompetent. In your case maybe she's jealous."

She didn't know if Iverson believed her or not. His expression never changed, and they looked at each other across the room steadily.

Finally Iverson moved, walking toward her. "Please stay with the Gerrick Corporation, Melissa. I promise that I won't smother you."

"I can't. I like it where I am."

"How long will you like it without my endorsement?"

She stared at him for a long time, disappointment causing her heart to ache. "With or without your endorsement, I'll stay. I think we'll do very well without it. I think, though, Iverson, you'd better go to your office and do some cleaning up, or you'll never find a suitable administrative assistant no matter what agency you go through." She eyed him levelly. "Believe it or not, Ramona Swinson is your own worst enemy."

Still he made no comment, and Melissa shrugged.

She had said all she could. Now it was up to him. She picked up the coats and sweaters, draped them across her arm, and walked across the room, her hand closing over the doorknob.

"Melissa," Iverson called softly, "it's me or Day's Work. I've had one wife who put her firm first, and I won't have another."

Melissa turned. "I love you, and I want to marry you, but I refuse to be bound by your fears, Iverson. You must realize I'm not Nicole; I'm not like Nicole." She lifted a hand, pushing her glasses up her nose. "I'm sorry that you haven't seen that for yourself. I like my job at Day's Work, and I wish to keep it until such time that I want to quit. Not before." She tried to reach him; she tried to burrow under his fears and his anger. "I don't love it more than I love you, nor is it going to be my top priority." She shifted the wraps from one arm to the other. "If I had my way, Iverson, I would ask that you stop the negotiations with Whitman and Dillson because I don't want you around Nicole, but I'm not. Nor am I going to ask that you give up the Gerrick Corporation. I'm not making any of these requests a condition for marriage."

"Melissa." He spoke very quietly, and it seemed that he hadn't even heard her words. "Please don't go. Don't leave me."

"I'm not leaving you." She turned the doorknob. "I'm just going home with Mom tonight to let you think things over."

"If you change your mind," he said, "call me."

"No," she said, moving through the door, "if *you* change *your* mind, you call me."

She walked into the living room and passed out the wraps, draping her stole around her shoulders, joining in the laughter and the good-byes. Smiling brightly,

182

she turned to Linda when everyone was bundled up, ready to get a ride home with Penny and Charlie.

"I'm going home now. You can ride with me if you wish," Melissa said.

Everyone was taken aback, and the silence was stretching thin when Linda finally asked, "All right, but what about Iverson?"

Melissa's smile widened, but if Linda had looked more closely at Melissa's eyes, she would have seen the mist of tears. "He's going to have to work tonight since he's goofed off the weekend with me."

The explanation seemed to satisfy the group, and the noise of departure began once again. Iverson walked them to the porch, but he went no farther. However, when the van drove away, he stood watching, his heart breaking. And though he looked composed, he was crying inside.

Knowing she had to give Iverson time to think, Melissa drove home and sat up the rest of the night in the living room, unable to sleep. Deep down she hoped that Iverson would call, but he didn't. Just before sunrise she awakened her mother, telling her that she was taking the day off and was going off to be by herself.

Without taking the time to change her clothes, Melissa climbed into the van that hadn't been unpacked since their trip to Cherokee, and she began to drive, seeking a peaceful refuge. When she arrived at the Mount Haven Inn, Miss Mary Jane and Mr. R. L. asked about Iverson, but when she replied, "It's just me this time," they questioned her no more. Getting her small bag out of the van, she walked to the cabin and quickly changed into her jeans and shirt, and, undisturbed, she wandered around the mountainside all day, spending a great portion of the time at the church.

Now she sat in the quiet solitude of the mountain

cabin, her only light the flickering glow of the small lamp on the mantel. She could have turned on the overhead light, but she preferred this. Sighing deeply, she turned her head, looking at the delicate lace blouse that lay on the bed, remembering the happiness she had felt when she had dressed for dinner at Orlaine's.

Several times during the night Iverson picked up the phone and dialed Melissa's number, but just before it rang, he always hung up. He paced back and forth. He even went so far as to get in his car, but he didn't turn the key. Slowly, wearily, he closed the car door and went back inside.

Why did he hesitate? he wondered. Too proud or too cowardly? Did he really expect her to come groveling on her knees when he was the one who owed her an apology? Dear God, no! That's what he loved about Melissa. Her strength.

She was right. She wasn't Nicole, and she wasn't like Nicole. She was Melissa Phillips, the woman whom he wanted to marry, the woman whom he wanted to spend the rest of his life with. If she had been like Nicole, he wouldn't love her. She had every right to her career and to the job of her choice. Selfishly he had wanted her with him, so he could control her. Because he had been thinking only of himself and not of her, he hadn't considered her feelings at all.

By morning he made his decision. Life without Melissa wasn't worth living. He rushed out of the house, running to the car, and he drove directly to her house. He rang the doorbell with one hand and pounded on the door with the other, getting Linda out of bed.

"Good morning," she greeted him sleepily, stifling a yawn with her hand.

"May I speak with Melissa?" His voice was gruff with nervous apprehension.

"If she were here, you could," Linda replied, "but she's not. She left before daybreak, and—"

"Where is she?" he demanded, raking his hand over his beard-stubbled face.

"I don't know. She didn't tell me where she was going. She said she would call me later and let me know." Iverson's face crumpled, and he exhaled deeply. "I'm sorry," she murmured.

"Did she give you a clue of any kind?" Iverson demanded, the russet eyes scouring her face for evidence.

Linda shook her head, trying to remember. "She said she wanted to get away to think. Something about heaven, or haven." She wrinkled her brow, frowning as she summoned the hazy thoughts. "Something about rest."

Iverson's frown cleared. Running down the sidewalk to his car, he called over his shoulder. "Thanks, Mrs. Cresswell, and don't worry. I know where she is."

"I hope so," Linda shouted, fully awake now, watching as he screeched out of her driveway.

Melissa sat beneath the dogwood tree, her knees drawn to her chest, her arms wrapped around them. Despite her disagreement with Iverson, she felt at peace with the world, and she knew that the time she had spent up here had been good for her. Truly this mountain had become her haven, her place of refuge. As the wind rustled through the trees, she stared at the small cemetery; then she looked at the white frame church. Finally she closed her eyes, enjoying the warmth of the sunshine, slipping into a near sleep.

She didn't open her eyes again until she felt his shadow as it fell across her. "Hi," she said, knowing that it was he without even looking. "I've been waiting."

"Sorry I couldn't get here any sooner," he told her, sitting down, picking up a twig between his fingers, "but after I figured out where you were, I went to the office and did some housecleaning." He crossed his legs in front of himself and leaned back against the tree trunk next to Melissa. "I spoke to Ramona Swinson and found out that she was sabotaging you and other new help. I suppose she thought she could make herself seem indispensable to me. Or maybe it was just pure jealousy."

"And?" Melissa asked, slowly opening her eyes.

"I have two vacancies to fill now, administrative assistant and personal secretary."

"Going through an agency for replacements?" she asked quietly.

"Thought I would," he returned absently, lying down beside her. "Can you recommend a good one?"

"I've heard that Day's Work is pretty good," she replied with no show of emotion, picking a blade of grass and pulling it through her lips.

"Seems I've heard about that one before. Tell me something about them."

"Well," she said, pretending to be in deep thought, "I've heard they're the tops. Good employees, and you ought to see the manager. While she's not a raving beauty, I'm told that she's a knockout." She grinned.

"She is for a fact," he agreed somberly, his eyes on her face. "She's completely knocked me out." He broke the twig between his fingers and tossed it away. "I don't think I'll ever get over the blow."

"Do you want to?"

"Don't think I do," he returned, rolling over. Gently he reached out a hand and pulled her glasses off, folding the ear pieces, dropping them into his shirt pocket. Then he pulled her into his arms. "I love you, Melissa." The beautiful, heartfelt words were whisper-

186

soft, brushing happiness over her soul. "More deeply than you can imagine."

"I know," she whispered. "That's how I love you. So much that I would sooner die than live without you."

"I'm sorry," he apologized. "Sorry that I hurt you and that I issued that stupid ultimatum. I was"—he hesitated, his words thick—"I was afraid of losing you, baby. So afraid, that I was going to keep you by my side day and night."

"I understand," she murmured.

"Now I realize that I would have suffocated you, in turn suffocating our love and ultimately killing what I so wanted to cherish and to protect." His arms tightened about her, and he buried his face in the softness of her shoulder. "Can you forgive me, darling?"

Melissa moved her fingertip lovingly over that rugged, angular face. "I forgive you, darling, because I love you the same way."

"The old proverb is so true, darling," he mused. "If you love something, you must give it freedom and room to grow."

She smiled. "Perhaps because we love this deeply and this greatly we'll never take each other for granted."

"I hope so," he said, hugging her, thanking God for having given him one more chance. "I'll spend the rest of my life proving my love to you. You're my life."

Melissa chuckled. "Good, because I've been planning our wedding."

"The Haven of Rest?"

She nodded. "What do you think?"

"I can't think of a better place."

They laughed together, their joy echoing through the forest.

187

All-new
Candlelight Newsletter

**An exceptional,
free offer awaits readers
of Dell's incomparable Candlelight Ecstasy and Supreme Romances.**

Subscribe to our all-new CANDLELIGHT NEWSLETTER and you will receive—at absolutely no cost to you—exciting, exclusive information about today's finest romance novels and novelists. You'll be part of a select group to receive sneak previews of upcoming Candlelight Romances, well in advance of publication.

You'll also go behind the scenes to "meet" our Ecstasy and Supreme authors, learning firsthand where they get their ideas and how they made it to the top. News of author appearances and events will be detailed, as well. And contributions from the Candlelight editor will give you the inside scoop on how she makes her decisions about what to publish—and how *you* can try your hand at writing an Ecstasy or Supreme.

You'll find all this and more in Dell's CANDLELIGHT NEWSLETTER. And best of all, *it costs you nothing*. That's right! It's Dell's way of thanking our loyal Candlelight readers and of adding another dimension to your reading enjoyment.

Just fill out the coupon below, return it to us, and look forward to receiving the first of many CANDLELIGHT NEWSLETTERS—overflowing with the kind of excitement that only enhances our romances!

**DELL READERS SERVICE – Dept. B430A
P.O. BOX 1000, PINE BROOK, N.J. 07058**

Name_____

Address_____

City_____

State_____ Zip_____

Candlelight
Ecstasy Romances™

$1.95 each

Candlelight
Ecstasy Romances™

$1.95 each